"I'm sorry, Mac. This isn't going to happen."

It took a long second for her words to sink in. Then he said, "All right. Can you tell me why?"

"I just—a lot of reasons."

He was entitled to an explanation, but she couldn't tell him Charles would kill her if she ever let another man touch her. *I'll know if you betray me, Erin. I have many friends…and they have many friends. You belong to me. You will always belong to me.*

She met the confusion in Mac's eyes again. How could she tell him anything about her life with Charles and keep his respect? More to the point, how could she tell him anything, period? Her attraction to him went beyond anything she'd ever felt for a man, but he was still very much a stranger to her. She'd only known him for two weeks, and it took longer than that to establish trust. Her daughter had to be her first priority. One innocent word to the wrong person could turn their lives into a living hell.

Dear Reader,

What better way to start off a new year than with six terrific new Silhouette Intimate Moments novels? We've got miniseries galore, starting with Karen Templeton's *Staking His Claim*, part of THE MEN OF MAYES COUNTY. These three brothers are destined to find love, and in this story, hero Cal Logan is also destined to be a father—but first he has to convince heroine Dawn Gardner that in his arms is where she wants to stay.

For a taste of royal romance, check out Valerie Parv's *Operation: Monarch*, part of THE CARRAMER TRUST, crossing over from Silhouette Romance. Policemen more your style? Then check out Maggie Price's *Hidden Agenda*, the latest in her LINE OF DUTY miniseries, set in the Oklahoma City Police Department. Prefer military stories? Don't even try to resist *Irresistible Forces,* Candace Irvin's newest SISTERS IN ARMS novel. We've got a couple of great stand-alone books for you, too. Lauren Nichols returns with a single mom and her protective hero, in *Run to Me*. Finally, Australian sensation Melissa James asks *Can You Forget?* Trust me, this undercover marriage of convenience will stick in your memory long after you've turned the final page.

Enjoy them all—and come back next month for more of the best and most exciting romance reading around, only in Silhouette Intimate Moments.

Yours,

Leslie J. Wainger
Executive Editor

Please address questions and book requests to:
Silhouette Reader Service
U.S.: 3010 Walden Ave., P.O. Box 1325, Buffalo, NY 14269
Canadian: P.O. Box 609, Fort Erie, Ont. L2A 5X3

Run to Me
LAUREN NICHOLS

Silhouette®

INTIMATE MOMENTS™

Published by Silhouette Books

America's Publisher of Contemporary Romance

SILHOUETTE BOOKS

ISBN 0-373-27341-X

RUN TO ME

Visit Silhouette at www.eHarlequin.com

Printed in U.S.A.

Books by Lauren Nichols

Silhouette Intimate Moments

Accidental Heiress #840
Accidental Hero #893
Accidental Father #994
Bachelor in Blue Jeans #1164
Run to Me #1271

LAUREN NICHOLS

started writing by accident, so it seems fitting that the word *accidental* appears in her first three titles for Silhouette. Once eager to illustrate children's books, she tried to get her foot in that door, only to learn that most publishing houses used their own artists. Then one publisher offered to look at her sketches if she also wrote the tale. During the penning of that story, Lauren fell head over heels in love with writing fiction.

In addition to her novels, Lauren's romance and mystery short stories have appeared in several leading magazines. She counts her family and friends as her greatest treasures, and strongly believes in the Beatles' philosophy, "All You Need Is Love." When this Pennsylvania author isn't writing or trying unsuccessfully to give up French vanilla cappuccino, she's traveling or hanging out with her very best friend/husband, Mike.

Lauren loves to hear from her readers. You can contact her at http:www.laurennichols.com.

I was blessed with four great brothers
but was never lucky enough to have a sister,
so this book is dedicated to my sisters of the heart—
the terrific women who make my days more fun with
their friendships, e-mails, phone calls, promises of
prayers and, frequently, the threat of
a three-mile walk to get me in shape
(which is a lost cause).

For the one and only Anna Banana.
For Karen Rose, Doreen, Shirley, Lisa and Gladys.

For my Looper pals:
Ann, Jacki, Jan, Liana, Lorraine, Polly and Susan.

I love you guys.

And always for Mike,
for taking such good care of my wimpy heart.

Chapter 1

The lies were getting easier to tell.

Hiding a stab of guilt, Erin Fallon carried her nearly three-year-old daughter out of Amos Perkins's sturdy clapboard home to his porch, then held the wooden screen door for Amos. Once, a lie would have died on her tongue; her father's cheating had hurt her mother so badly, Erin grew up with a deep respect for the truth. But for the past year, honesty had had to take a back seat to survival.

Christie's warm breath and sweet baby whisper bathed Erin's ear. "I'n firsty, Mommy."

"We'll get some juice in a minute, sweetheart," she returned quietly, then shifted her attention back to her new employer.

Amos winced with exertion as he stepped over the threshold and onto the porch, then drew a few labored breaths. He continued the conversation they'd begun inside the house. "Then yer okay with the pay?"

"It's more than generous, Mr. Perkins. Thank you." The money was a godsend. Buying the first van had seriously depleted her funds, then, when in fear, she'd traded the white Ford Windstar in on an older vehicle, there'd been no refund. Not that she cared. Now she had an anonymous-looking gray van that few people would notice.

"'Course, your room and meals are included," Amos continued, his wispy gray hair lifting in the early-June breeze. His cane thumped hollowly on the plank floor as he moved past two Adirondack chairs and an old green-and-yellow glider to brace himself against a porch post. "How soon can you ladies start?"

Alarmed that he would lose his footing so close to the steps, Erin put Christie down and wandered to Amos's side. "As soon as you like. Everything we need is in the van."

His startled look drew a smile from Erin. "Christie and I travel light, Mr. Perkins."

"Call me Amos. And I s'pose now's as good a time as any to start." He nodded down the sloping hill to his right, indicating an old but well-kept barn, a split-rail corral and two small outbuildings. Beyond them a pasture stretched to meet a wall of Ponderosa pines, and in the distance the majestic San Francisco peaks rose triumphantly against the summer-blue sky.

"Like I said," he repeated, "it ain't much of a ranch. We run a few steers and horses for our own use. Couple-a cats to keep the mice busy."

Christie clung to her leg, and Erin reached down to stroke her fine black hair. "It's beautiful here."

"We like it." Amos's brow furrowed. "You should know, not much happens here in High Hawk. We're a whole twenty miles from Flagstaff—don't have none of them nightclubs like you folks have back East. That gonna be a problem for you?''

Erin nearly laughed at the irony. After the scare they'd had in Maine, they desperately wanted and needed the seclusion. ''Not at all. Christie and I like it quiet.''

''Good. You'll get a lot of that here.'' He jabbed his cane to the left, indicating the fairly new, light-golden-brown log home she'd noticed when she'd arrived. It was less than a hundred yards away, surrounded by trees and greenery, and separated from Amos's home by a small, sun-spangled pond. ''Go ahead and move your stuff into my grandson's place.'' A faint grumble entered his tone. ''Lord knows he ain't usin' it. Since my stroke, he's been hauntin' *my* house.''

Amos's tone evened out. ''You'll have more room over there, anyways. When we advertised for a live-in housekeeper, we didn't figure on a young'un. Truth is,'' he went on, ''this housekeeper nonsense is *his* idea. I did just fine before the stroke, and I do just fine now.''

Erin smiled, but she could see that wasn't so. Though his folksy speech hadn't been affected—or if it had, he'd recovered—Amos's right leg was weak, and the responsibility of running his general store in addition to his home chores was undoubtedly more than he could handle.

She glanced again at the sprawling log home with its deep wraparound porch, suddenly uneasy. ''Mr.... Amos. Are you sure your grandson's all right with us staying in his home? That is, did you mention it when you phoned him earlier?''

"If the boy's gonna insist I get another housekeeper, he'll hafta put up with the rest of it."

"Then...I'm the second? Third?" And what had happened to her predecessors?

"Second and last," Amos grumbled again. "First one had her cap set for me. I wasn't interested."

The roar of a rapidly approaching vehicle drew their attention, and Amos squinted toward the dirt road beyond his driveway. A moment later an old, pale blue truck with an emblem on its side appeared, trailing a plume of dust as it sped toward the house.

"Speak of the devil," Amos said through a low chuckle. "Figured he'd hightail it back here soon as I phoned and told him to take down the Help Wanted sign at the store."

"Your grandson?" Erin asked, unnerved as the truck came to a skidding, gravel-spraying stop behind her van. This wasn't the arrival of a passive, agreeable man, she thought, her heart sinking. This man was churned up about something—and it was probably her. Suddenly she wondered if she could count on this job after all.

"Mac," Amos replied, pride in his hazel eyes. "My daughter Jessie's boy, God rest her soul."

The broad-shouldered man who swung out of the truck was tall, tanned and so beautifully put together that for an instant everything in Erin stilled. The black Stetson he wore low on his brow covered most of his dark-brown hair, and his chambray shirt, rolled back over muscular forearms, was open throated, showing a hint of chest hair. As he moved unerringly toward her, Erin's gaze dipped to the faded jeans that hugged his thighs and calves...and she drew a soft breath.

At her short-lived job in Maine, the pretty teenage

waitress she'd worked with had had a word for men like him—men who brought a flush to her cheeks and sent her scurrying to their tables to take their orders. She could almost hear Trisha's flirty whisper now. *Smokin'*.

But as Amos's grandson crossed the weed-choked grass, giving her a critical once-over, another word occurred to Erin. *Trouble*. It was obvious from his long strides and body language that he didn't approve of his grandfather's choice in housekeepers, and he meant to do something about it.

Backing away from the steps, Erin lifted Christie into her arms again, turning her front and center. It wasn't terribly noble to use her daughter as a bargaining chip, but when they were fighting for their lives, she'd use whatever weapons she had. Christie's blue eyes and shy smile had totally disarmed Amos. His grandson would be a harder sell.

"Hello," he said politely as he ascended the porch steps. "I'm Mac Corbett." The firm, callused hand he extended all but swallowed hers. "I understand Granddad's considering you for the housekeeper position."

"I ain't *considerin'* her," Amos snapped, "she's got the job. It's a done deal."

Frowning at his grandfather's precarious position, Corbett pulled a chair close and quietly asked Amos to sit. When Amos lifted his chin and belligerently stood his ground, the younger man sighed and dragged the chair between his granddad and the steps.

He worked up another smile and looked at Erin again. Christie promptly jammed her face into Erin's neck.

"You're okay," Erin murmured. "This is Mr. Corbett. He's a new friend."

Corbett extended his hand to her. "Can we shake?"

"No!" Christie shrieked.

"Honey, don't be rude."

"She's okay." Corbett's smile increased a little. "She has a right to pick her own friends." He drew a deep breath, then spoke again. "Would you excuse Granddad and me for a minute, Mrs.—"

"Terri Fletcher," she replied, praying Christie wouldn't correct this new lie. She'd spoken to her about their new names, but few toddlers were good at keeping secrets. "And it's Ms."

"Nice to meet you, Terri." He pulled open the screen door. "Granddad?" he prodded, glancing at Amos, then back at Erin. "We'll be right back. Feel free to walk around—check out the place."

"Thanks, we'll do that." Except, Erin knew that what he meant was, take a hike so I can grill my grandfather without being overheard. And she had a very good idea what he would say. We don't know her. How can we trust her? Maybe Corbett even had someone else in mind for the position. All she knew was, whatever his motive for this *tête à tête,* the big man was miffed at being left out of the hiring loop. Seeing the return of that grim expression as he ushered Amos inside, Erin decided with a heavy heart that her chances of staying here were slim to none.

When the inside door as well as the screen door banged shut, she sighed and walked Christie to the van to grab a box of apple juice from the cooler and the local paper from the front seat. Hopefully, another look at the want ads would turn up something more promising. If not…they'd be moving on again.

Clamping the paper beneath her arm, she popped the attached straw into the juice box and handed the drink to Christie. "Here you go, sweetie pie. Now, what do you say?"

"*Danka!*"

Chills erupted on Erin's skin.

Slowly she crouched down to Christie's level, laid the paper aside, and dredged up a smile, meeting her daughter's sparkling blue eyes. "No, sweetheart, we say, 'thank you,' when someone gives us a treat. Remember? Can you say it for me now?"

"Fank you," she repeated happily, innocently unaware of what she'd done to her mother.

"Good girl," Erin murmured and hugged her close, juice box and all.

Her sober gaze found Amos Perkins's home again, and she wondered what was being said in there. She didn't blame Mac Corbett for being cautious.

If he knew their past, he'd send them packing in a heartbeat.

Inside Amos's living room with its mismatched furniture and dated wallpaper, Mac faced his grandfather. He was still startled by the nerves twitching beneath his skin. Terri Fletcher was a dyed-in-the-wool knockout, and that was an understatement—even with her pretty black hair pulled back from her face in that tight ponytail. Even devoid of makeup. The shapeless, beige cotton shirt and slacks she wore only made him wonder what was beneath them—and why a woman that beautiful didn't want anyone to notice her.

Fat chance of that happening.

"Before you say one word," Amos began, stabbing a finger into Mac's chest, "I like her and she's stayin'. She's a nice woman, and she looks like she could use the money."

"I'm not disputing that, Granddad, I just would've liked to talk to her before we made a decision. What's her story? Has she done this kind of work before? What did her references say? Or didn't she offer any?"

Amos pulled a folded sheet of tablet paper from the breast pocket of his red-plaid flannel shirt. "Got 'em right here," he said defensively. "She checked out perfect."

"Did you even call them?" Mac reached for it. "How many references did she—"

Amos snatched the sheet away and stuffed it back in his pocket, his hazel eyes insulted and his lined face stubbornly set. "Since I got sick, you been callin' the shots—makin' my decisions for me—and it's time it stopped. There ain't nothin' wrong with my mind or my intuition, and I say she's fine."

Silent seconds ticked by while Mac pondered his grandfather's words. Then he nodded. Amos was right. He had been making all the decisions since the stroke. But everything he'd done, he'd done because he loved the old man. The last thing he'd wanted to do was hurt Amos's pride, but apparently, that's what he'd done.

"Okay. I'm sorry. It should be your decision. I just expected you to choose someone a little more… mature."

"You don't mean mature, you mean Mildred Manning."

"She was a nurse for years. It would've made more sense."

Amos stared as if Mac were completely out of his mind. "Don't you know nothin' about women?" He shook his head abruptly as though banishing a ridiculous notion, then answered his own question. "Never mind. 'Course you don't. If you did, you'd have one of yer own. Sophie'd be mad as a wet hen if I hired Mildred to cook and clean for me. 'Specially when she offered to do it herself. And don't tell me I ain't right about that.''

Releasing a weary blast of air, Mac brought his hands to his hips. Amos's wisecrack about his love life aside, the old guy had a point. Sophie Casselback was a good woman, but she would've made Amos's life a living hell if he'd hired a woman their age. She and Amos had been ''good friends'' for two years—the primary reason, Mac suspected, that Amos had refused her help. No man—even a seventy-three-year-old man—wanted to look less than strong around the woman he was keeping company with. Or maybe he and Sophie were over now. Since his stroke and stint in rehab, Amos hadn't returned many of her calls.

Amos continued to stare hard as Mac's thoughts churned off in yet another direction. ''Now what? There's something else goin' on under that hat. What is it?''

''The little girl,'' Mac said. ''Are you sure you'll be okay with a child underfoot? You could trip, you might not get your right rest—''

''You just got done sayin' it's my decision to make. I made it.'' Shuffling and cane tapping to the door, he threw it open, then shoved through the screen door, banging it against the white wood siding. Mac raised his eyes to heaven, but there was no help there. Obviously, the discussion was over.

Amos plopped himself down on the glider. ''Now why don't you help that gal take her stuff over to your place?''

''*My* place?''

''Little Christie needs some room, too. Can't very

well stuff 'em both in the guest room upstairs. Besides," Amos groused pointedly as Mac's exasperation grew, "*you* seem happy enough up there."

"Granddad, I'm not set up for company."

"They'll only be here six 'r seven weeks." Amos glared up at him. "Or do you have other ideas you ain't told me about?"

"No, but my guest room's full of boxes, and there's no bed in there." The other spare room had been turned into an office. That meant, if they moved in, Terri Fletcher and her daughter would be sleeping in his room.

In his bed.

Something tugged low in Mac's gut at the thought of Christie's slender mom beneath his sheets, startling him with its intensity and shocking the hell out of him by evoking a very physical, very unexpected response.

"All right," he growled, needing to move, and accepting the arrangement because there'd be no changing Amos's mind. "I'll get it done."

Erin followed Corbett's brisk strides through his spacious, beautiful home, her stomach a ball of knots. She was astonished that the discussion had ended in her favor. Initially, he'd seemed to be the man in control, yet somehow Amos had won out. Relieved, Erin sent up a prayer of thanks that they had a roof over their heads again—and on the heels of that prayer, another went up that changing her name and relocating here would be enough to ensure their safety.

And incomprehensibly, amid so much turmoil, some part of her still found time to notice Mac Corbett as a man. Though she tried to ignore the pull, his rugged face and the smooth, loose way he walked made her feel things she hadn't felt in a very long time. In fact, he was the most overtly *male* man she'd ever encountered, and incredibly, he didn't seem aware of his appeal.

"Obviously, this is the bedroom," he said, carrying their bags inside and tossing them on his king-size bed. A quilted navy, white and light-blue spread in a geometric print covered it. "You should be comfortable here." He nodded at a closed door to the left of an oak chest of drawers. "Master bath's in there."

"It's very nice," she replied, placing the two duffels she'd carried beside her luggage. "Thank you. I...I'm sure we will be." She'd always been good at small talk, but with this man—who didn't seem inclined to make the effort—she was falling flat on her face.

Before they'd begun unloading the van, she'd given Christie her coloring book, crayons and a cookie, then settled her in the great room at Mac's distressed-pine coffee table. Occasionally, as they'd carted things past the wide archway, Christie had looked up from her tuneless humming and scribbling to peek through her fringe of black bangs and smile a little—beginning to adjust again. And though that was something to be thankful for, it still made Erin ache to see her take each new town and change of address in stride.

Suppressing a sigh, she shifted her attention back to Mac and tried again for conversation. "Christie's careful with her crayons, but I put a plastic play mat over your coffee table in case she gets reckless."

"It wasn't expensive," he said flatly. "She can't hurt it."

"Still, I want you to know that we'll leave your home in the same condition that we found it."

His polite smile thanked her, then he nodded at the

bare windows. "I never got around to putting up curtains. There didn't seem to be a big need for them, living out this far. But I guess you'll want some privacy. I'll see what I can scare up for you." He nodded at the bed. "The sheets are fresh, but you're welcome to change them. Linen closet's in the hall next to the family bath."

"I'm sure the sheets on the bed will be fine."

"All right, then I'll make room for your things so you can start putting them away. I'll finish unpacking your van in a minute." Crossing to his closet, he pulled a duffel bag from a shelf, then started filling it from the oak chest of drawers.

"Mr. Corbett?"

"Mac," he said, not looking up.

"Mac. First of all, you don't have to unpack my van. I can do that." Heaven knew she'd managed to do it enough times in the past year. "Secondly," she said, unable to keep the uneasiness from her voice, "I know you weren't expecting us to commandeer your home. So before we go much further—"

"You want to know if I have reservations."

"Yes."

His candid gaze met hers. "I do. Yes. But not about the two of you staying here." He resumed packing. "It's probably better that I sleep at Amos's anyway. Most of my clothes are there. I moved in right after he was released from rehab—" his mouth twisted in annoyance "—came back here after the first housekeeper was hired, then hauled butt back to Amos's when she left."

Mac emptied the next drawer, stuffing T-shirts into his bag. "Besides, sometimes he needs help getting to the bathroom in the middle of the night." He turned sharply to reassure her. ''Once he's up and moving in the morning, he's fine, though, so your duties won't be more than we advertised in the paper.''

''I don't have a problem helping your grandfather to the bathroom.''

His expression softened slightly, then he looked away again and zipped his bag, his tone brisk again. ''Thank you, but I was thinking of Amos. He has a lot of pride.''

''I noticed. And I'd never do anything to hurt it.''

''Good, because he's all I have, and that makes him my number-one priority. I don't like thinking he might be at risk—in any way.'' He met her eyes again. ''You do understand, don't you?''

Erin nodded. He didn't have to gush or expand on his statement. It was abundantly clear that he loved his granddad, and if Amos wasn't treated with care and respect, that Housekeeper Wanted sign would go right back up again.

Mac slung the duffel's long straps over his shoulder. ''I didn't see a crib or anything like it in your van. Christie sleeps with you?''

''Not always. Sometimes we find a furnished apartment with a twin bed. I have a portable safety railing that slides between the mattress and box spring. That works pretty well.''

''*Sometimes* you find a furnished apartment?'' he repeated in a tone that was cuttingly judgmental. ''Do you move around a lot?''

She knew she shouldn't feel defensive—he had a perfect right to question her—but she did. She also knew that antagonizing him could prompt another discussion between Mac and his grandfather, and this time the younger man might win.

"Is that a problem for you? This job *is* temporary, isn't it? Your grandfather said two months at the most, probably less."

The thoughts moving through his dark eyes weren't complimentary, and his face was carved granite. "Yes, it's temporary. I still find myself wondering why you're so mobile." His gaze delved more deeply into hers. "Maybe if I ask a few questions—get a few answers—I won't wonder so much."

He barely paused a moment before he said coolly, "Ms. Fletcher, are you running away from something?"

Chapter 2

She didn't know how she managed, but Erin spoke in a calm voice. "No. Are you afraid I'll take off in the middle of the night with the good silver?"

"I don't know. I don't know *you*."

Feeling a nervous flush creep into her cheeks, Erin turned away from him and began unpacking Christie's clothes. "Then let's remedy that right now. What do you want to know?" She was ready with her stock replies.

"All right. But keep in mind that this isn't a personal attack. I just need to feel comfortable with the people who take care of Amos."

"I understand. Go ahead."

"Your van has Maine plates. You don't have a Maine accent."

She shook the wrinkles out of Christie's pajamas and set them aside. "We were only there a short time."

"You were employed there?"

"Yes, I've already told your grandfa—"

"Doing what? And why did you leave?"

Erin put down the tiny bib overalls she'd just plucked from the suitcase, then turned around, realizing that her answers might be better accepted if she were facing him. She hid a shiver of apprehension. The penetrating eyes beneath the shading brim of his Stetson seemed to see straight through her. But as she gazed deeper into those eyes, past the concern, past the strength and confidence there, she saw something else. Something that mirrors had reflected in her own eyes. This man had baggage, too.

She drew a breath. "My last job was waitressing at a small restaurant. It was fun. I enjoy working with people." She got herself ready for the next lie. "I left because it took me away from Christie too many hours in the day."

"You had to travel 2500 miles to find a position that kept your daughter with you 24/7?"

"No, Maine was beautiful, but cold. I decided we'd be happier in a warmer climate."

"So you chose the *Flagstaff* area? Winters here can be—"

"This isn't our last stop. I've never seen California."

It was several seconds before he slowly nodded. Again the judgment and doubt in his dark gaze was a near palpable thing. "I assume you included the name and address of your previous employer in your list of references?"

"Yes." She'd only offered two names—Millie's and Lynn's—and thank heaven, they were both confidantes and prepared for phone calls. It still stunned her that Amos hadn't contacted either of them, saying that he was from the old school and judged people by the look in their eyes—and she looked all right to him. "Until last week I worked for Millie Kraft at Krafty Millie's Café in Spindrift, Maine, just up the coast from Boothbay Harbor. Your grandfather has her number. Is there anything else you'd like to know?"

Again, that long, slow gaze assessed her. But apparently the inquisition was over because he thanked her and walked out of the room. "There's a twin bed in storage at Granddad's house," he called over his shoulder. "I think I can squeeze it in here."

Erin trailed him through the hall toward the front door. "You don't have to do that. Christie will be fine, sleeping with me."

"She should have her own bed," he said firmly.

Suddenly Christie barreled out of the great room, a page from her coloring book flapping in her hand. Her tiny face was all smiles, her voice a high-pitched squeak. "*Wook,* Mommy!"

Smiling, Erin scooped Christie into her arms, then held the paper out in front of her. She gasped dramatically at the wild purple and yellow swirls and swishes. "Oh, my! Did you do this all by yourself?"

Christie nodded excitedly.

"It's beautiful. We'll have to dig out our magnets and put it on the refrigerator."

Heat rushed to her cheeks as Mac ambled back from the door. His deep voice gentled as he surveyed Christie's handiwork, the way most adults' voices did when speaking to a child. "Mommy's right. This is a very nice picture. Can you tell me what it is?"

"Me!"

"I can see that now," he replied chuckling. The

skin beside his dark eyes crinkled. "Do you think you could make one for my grandpa's refrigerator? I'll bet he'd like that. I know I would."

Beaming, Christie wriggled out of Erin's arms and raced back to her crayons.

Mac's gaze followed her. "How old is she?"

"Three. Well, she will be in three months. September."

"She's a cutie."

"Thank you. I think so."

His next words landed like a punch. "Her father must miss her very much."

It was hard to breathe, hard to remain calm, hard to hide the jolt of fear that now accompanied any thought or mention of Charles. But she made it through the moment without betraying any of those things and stated simply, "He's not with us anymore."

"He passed away?"

"Not to my knowledge."

When she didn't offer more, new questions rose in Corbett's eyes—curious questions—but apparently respecting her privacy, he didn't ask them. Instead, the look in his eyes slowly began to change.

The difference was subtle, almost unnoticeable…but for the shortest of seconds, his gaze passed over her hair and the slope of her face—lingered for a heartbeat on her mouth. And Erin's pulse quickened as awareness came tiptoeing back, all the more potent because they were alone, behind closed doors, and she now realized the attraction was mutual.

Time stretched out on tenterhooks.

The air between them quivered with a tension running just below the surface.

Then Mac abruptly jerked his gaze from hers and

retraced his steps to the door. "I'll see about that bed," he said brusquely, exiting and closing the screen door behind him.

"Th-thank you again for your trouble," Erin called.

"It's no trouble. As I said," he repeated, his growling baritone trailing, "she needs her own bed."

Erin sank back against a polished pine wall. Their search for a safe haven was over. In a month or two they might have to look again, but they were all right for now. She stared through the screen at Mac's broad shoulders and tapering back as he cut through the weeds bordering the pond on his way back to Amos's...took in his trim hips and long muscular legs.

And suddenly she wondered if she'd traded one kind of danger for another.

Charles Fallon sat behind the antique desk in his opulent high-rise office, the glow of the setting sun coloring the Chicago skyline behind him. He adjusted the pocket silk in his Armani suit, smoothed his fine mustache and goatee, then steepled his fingers before him and called, "Come in" in answer to the soft rap at his door.

A good-looking young man with longish, sun-streaked blond hair and a pleasant smile entered and walked to Charles's desk, his running shoes silent on the deep-orchid carpeting. He wore jeans and a white polo shirt with a sports logo on the breast pocket, and while he was not muscular, he appeared fit. He did not offer to shake Charles's hand, and they did not exchange pleasantries.

They were alone on the floor. Everyone who worked for him here at Fallon Financial Consultants had gone for the day.

With an economy of motion, Charles took a folder from his desk and handed it to John Smith. It contained photographs and every scrap of information Charles could recall or gather that might lead Smith to her. Her pathetic little hobbies and interests, her education, the foods she liked. Still on Charles's desk were her high school yearbook and a list of friends and associates she'd made at the elementary school where she'd once taught kindergarten. There was even a list of her e-mail contacts.

Several minutes elapsed while Smith studied the folder, the only sound in the room the hollow bubbling of the aquarium built into the cherry-paneled north wall. Presently Smith glanced up from the private detective's report. "She was last seen near Boothbay Harbor driving a 1999 white Ford Windstar?"

"Read on. The vehicle is current, but my private investigator frightened her into running again. He was able to pick up her trail but lost her again in Boston. He said she obviously knew she was being followed, the way she changed lanes and used the on and off ramps." So unlike his mousy little wife, who'd rarely driven in city traffic.

The square-cut diamond on his right hand caught the setting sun's rays as Charles flicked a hand at the folder. "It's all in there."

Charles stared at the boy-man as he continued to peruse the file. He was thirty years old, and his name was not Smith. But Charles didn't want or need to know what it was. He only had to know that Smith was short on scruples, long on patience, and used whatever means he deemed appropriate—legal or not—to accomplish his assignments. Which would make him far more effective than the fool who'd lost her.

Smith paged back to the photos. "Your ex-wife's very beautiful. Little girl looks just like her."

Charles nodded stiffly, hiding his rage as their faces coalesced in his mind. Beautiful, duplicitous Erin, with her serious cobalt eyes and raven hair, courtesy of the black Irish father who'd never given a damn about her. And Christiana. What an insult that none of his features had been repeated in his daughter's face. *He* was the strong one. *His* genes should have been dominant. *She should have had auburn hair and green eyes.*

He thought of the divorce in which Erin had aired their private differences—differences *every* man and wife had—and the absurd judgment that had awarded her full custody because the judge considered him abusive, unfit.

Her lies had made him a pariah with friends and associates. If she'd remained silent, he could've forgiven her her fanciful request for a divorce. Not granted it, but in time, forgiven it. Now…now she would pay.

"You know what I want," Charles said coldly, standing and bringing the meeting to a close. He placed the yearbook and lists inside a messenger's pouch, then indicated with a nod that Smith should add the folder he held, as well. When he'd complied, Charles handed him an envelope containing thirty thousand dollars.

"Half now, half when the job is done."

"Plus expenses."

"Of course." Charles held Smith's gaze. "Don't do it in front of my daughter. When you've finished, call me."

"I'll be in touch," the young man replied, smiling cordially and accepting the pouch.

Charles smiled back. *"Danka."*

Erin wiped the tomato sauce from Christie's mouth and hands, then lifted her down from the booster seat. She handed her her Raggedy Ann doll and a cookie. Ten feet away, in the spare room, the rattle and clank of metal framework told her that Mac would soon be finished assembling the twin bed he'd found in Amos's attic. And she was grateful. She wanted him gone so her popping nerve endings would give her some peace.

Mustering a smile, she led Christie around the butcher block island in the middle of the spacious kitchen to a bright, multiwindowed corner where a few toys and books lay on her open Barbie sleeping bag. "Can you read your dolly a story for a few minutes until Mommy rinses the dishes? We mustn't bother Mr. Corbett while he's working." She also didn't want her getting hurt.

Ignoring Erin's protests, Mac had decided that Christie not only needed her own bed, but her own room—even though it meant transferring a dozen sealed boxes to his computer room. Even though Erin reminded him they wouldn't be here very long.

"Can Waggedy Ann have a cookie?"

Erin smiled. "No, Waggedy Ann is too messy. When I'm through we'll do something fun, okay?"

"Okay, Mommy."

Another thud came from the spare room. Drawing a shaky breath, Erin carried their lunch dishes—their very late lunch dishes—to the sink, amazed that she'd managed to gag down a peanut butter and jelly sandwich with Mac here. Christie'd had no problem at all with the small, microwavable container of macaroni and meat sauce from their bag of staple groceries.

She was running water in the sink and rinsing the milk film from Christie's plastic cup when a deep male voice directly behind her said, "That should do it." The cup flew from her hands, popping and rattling hollowly against gleaming stainless steel.

Hating her over-the-top reaction to him, she shut off the water and turned to face him. "Thank you. Again."

"You're welcome. Again." He grinned down at Christie, who was chattering something unintelligible and grinding her cookie into Raggedy Ann's painted mouth, then spoke to Erin again.

"I left a set of twin sheets and a couple of blankets from Granddad's house on the bed. They're clean, and the mattress was stored in a spare room, so it's not musty smelling."

His hat was gone now, and his dark-brown hair was mussed and...sexy looking. "Thanks," she said, jerking her mind back where it belonged.

Mac waved off her gratitude, then strode to the refrigerator to check the crisper and meat drawers. In a moment he closed it again. "The only perishables in there are apples, and they look okay. Feel free to use them, and whatever you need from the cupboards."

"That's very kind," Erin murmured, "but we pay our own way." Wiping her hands on a paper towel, she looked for a wastebasket. Blood rushed to her face when he took it from her and deposited it in a stainless steel receptacle built into a lower cabinet.

"Your grandfather said he'd like me to start work tomorrow. Is that your understanding, too?"

"Yes. I'll handle the meal tonight, but I'd appreciate

it if you'd be at Amos's by eight in the morning. I gave Martin—Martin Trumbull, our full-time clerk—the rest of the week off. He's been putting in some long hours since the first housekeeper left, and he's no spring chicken.''

At last, a familiar topic of conversation. ''You mean the housekeeper who was interested in your grandfather?'' she asked with a faint smile. ''He said she'd…what was it? Set her cap for him?''

''That would've been nice if it had been true.''

''It's not?''

''Amos tends to give answers he's comfortable with,'' he answered, then changed the subject. ''There was no mention of it in our newspaper ad, but would you be able to drive him to his physical therapy sessions when I can't get away from the store? We have two part-time high-school kids who help out, but I don't like to leave them alone if I can help it.''

''Of course. Just give me directions. I'm not familiar with the area yet.''

''You're sure? He has PT on Tuesdays and Fridays. I can take him tomorrow, but we're expecting a fairly large shipment on Friday, and I need to be there to unload it. I don't want Martin or the kids hoisting eighty-pound feed sacks.''

''I'm sure.'' But she frowned suddenly, wondering if there might be a problem. ''Will your grandfather be able to step up into my van?''

''Not without help. There's a hydraulic lift that adjusts to any level off the back porch. I had it installed so he could ride in my Cherokee. Just steady him as he's getting in.'' Mac sighed wearily. ''If he'll let you. I prefer driving him myself so I can see and hear first-hand how he's doing, but since I can't, I'd appreciate it if you'd pay close attention to what—''

He stopped himself, massaged the furrows over his eyebrows. ''Never mind, I can phone his therapist. As for directions, the hospital's not hard to find. Amos can direct you.'' He met her eyes. ''Okay?''

It took that moment and that worn look to see that Amos's illness had taken a very large toll on his grandson, too. ''How long has it been since his stroke?'' Erin asked quietly.

''Ten months.''

''That's a long time.''

''Yeah. It's been a long haul for him.'' He glanced around as though he might say something else, but then his lips thinned. ''I'd better get back. I don't like leaving him alone for too long.''

Hopping up from her puffy nest, Christie ran after them, and automatically Erin took her hand as they went to the door. But her thoughts were still on Mac. It had to be a strain, putting your life on hold to tend to another person's needs, no matter how much you loved them. Although, she sensed this man wouldn't have it any other way. Handing his home over to strangers probably wasn't helping his peace of mind, either.

''See you in the morning, Terri,'' he said, closing the screen door and heading for the steps.

''See you. Thanks again for setting up the bed.''

Then, out of the blue, Christie delivered a giggling announcement that drove the air from Erin's lungs and threatened to dump her on the floor.

Slowly Mac reversed directions, his dark eyes sharp again. He repeated Christie's innocently spoken words. ''Terri is Mommy's *new* name?''

Blood thudding in her temples, Erin scrambled hard for another lie. It came to her like manna from heaven. Swinging Christie into her arms, she laughed, "Not 'new' name, sweetheart, *nick*name." She grinned wryly at Mac. "We had a talk this morning about the names we use being short for our given names. Apparently, she got things a little mixed up."

But Christie's little brow was still lined in confusion, and her rosebud lips were opening. Before she could breathe another syllable, Erin peppered her face and neck with noisy kisses that started Christie squirming and shrieking at the top of her lungs. "And now that you have a bed, Lady Jane," she teased over the noise, "it's time for your nap."

"I'n not Wady Jane!"

"Shouldn't that be your new nickname?"

"No!"

"Okay," Erin agreed over the pounding of her heart. "I like the old one better anyway."

When her daughter's giggles had dissolved into a sparkling smile, Erin faced Mac again, praying desperately that he believed the performance he'd just witnessed.

He seemed to.

"If you need to reach us at Amos's, use the intercoms. There's one in my room, one at the desk in the computer room, and one just inside the great room. Just press the button and speak."

"I'll do that, thank you." But as he climbed inside the old blue truck and drove off, she knew she wouldn't. There was no point in giving him an opportunity to ask more questions.

Easing Christie back a bit, Erin released a lung-clearing sigh and touched the tip of her nose to her daughter's. "Okay, chatterbox, let's get a sip of juice and visit the potty, then take that nap, okay?"

"Are you ezausted, Mommy?"

Erin smiled wanly. "You have no idea how exhausted I am, precious girl."

She considered having another talk with her about their new last name, but thought better of it. To tell her again that it was a secret that only they could know might confuse her all the more—and might invite yet another knee-buckling announcement. As the old adage went, it was best to let sleeping dogs lie.

Fifteen minutes later, with Christie curled warmly against her and softly snoring, Erin stared up at the ceiling from Mac's bed. Varnished pine tiles in various sizes and shapes formed a lovely mosaic overhead and met smooth, pine plank walls, just as they did in the rest of the house.

They were in. They'd passed the test. They had a job and a home until Amos no longer needed them. And Christie... Gazing down at her slumbering child, Erin felt a rush of emotion that brought tears to her eyes and thickened her chest. Christie was happy and secure, now. There were no longer any signs of anxiety or fear. No furious thumb sucking, no cries in the middle of the night. She stroked her daughter's glossy hair, smoothed back several damp strands from her temple and cheek.

Children should never be afraid.

Between household duties and keeping Christie entertained, Tuesday morning and afternoon flew by smoothly. The only glitch happened at breakfast when Mac walked into the kitchen, fresh from his shower in a hunter-green oxford shirt and snug jeans. But he only stayed long enough to shatter her composure, tell Amos to be ready at one o'clock for his appointment, and say goodbye. The butterflies that had gathered in Erin's stomach left through the same screen door.

It was nearly six o'clock when Amos shuffled into the living room to his recliner and the evening paper, and Erin started the dishes. She'd pushed two vintage, chrome and red-vinyl kitchen chairs together so Christie could stand beside her at the double-bowl sink and "help."

Christie was butchering a nursery rhyme and dumping water from a plastic cup to a metal pan when Mac walked up behind them, nearly soundless in his stocking feet. He slipped his coffee cup into the frothy soap bubbles, and his warm arm grazed Erin's. "Supper was delicious," he murmured. "Thank you."

Chills of awareness drizzled from the nape of her neck to the soles of Erin's feet. Like a second shadow, the heat emanating from his body warmed her side and back.

"You're welcome. I figured I couldn't go wrong with chicken." She hazarded a brief glance over her shoulder at him. He was standing so close, she could count every whisker in his end-of-day stubble, detect the faintest hint of a musky aftershave.

Her gaze rebounded to the plate she was washing. "The two of you left so quickly this afternoon, I didn't have time to suggest a menu."

"We eat anything," he returned, settling a hip against the cabinet. "We're not fussy."

"Still, you could have had a choice. What do you prefer?"

As she rinsed the plate and stacked it in the drainer to her left, Erin glanced at Christie. The front of her daughter's pink-and-white shirt was drenched, and water slopped over the side of the pan as she stirred "water soup" with a big plastic spoon.

"Since Amos's stroke, we've been trying to eat meals that are a little healthier." He laughed softly, and his warm breath somehow carried to her neck. Or maybe she just imagined it. "Which only means," he continued, "that I bought a bunch of those TV dinners with less fat and more vegetables."

"I saw them in the freezer. I can serve those for lunch if your granddad likes them. I could also look for some reduced fat recipes—" a convenient thought struck her as she finished "—on the Internet."

In time, she'd planned to ask a favor of him, but now that she had an opening, there was no point in putting it off. She hoped she wasn't too early with the request.

Swallowing, she rinsed their silverware, placed it in the drainer's cup and turned to face him. The sheer height and breadth of him still took some getting used to. He had to be six-two without his boots, seven full inches taller than she was.

"I have a laptop with a modem," she began hesitantly. "But I won't be here long enough to make subscribing to an Internet provider worthwhile. I was wondering if—"

He seemed to read her mind. "No problem. You're welcome to use the computer in my office."

"Thanks. Do you have any objection to my e-mailing a friend from time to time? I'll pay any charges, of course."

"There won't be any. I have a local server. Just let me know when you want to use it. I'll type in my password."

Feeling like a child asking permission to do something wrong, Erin nodded her acceptance, then summoned a shaky smile. "Not to press the issue, but if you have a moment later, the sooner I dig up some recipes, the healthier you and your granddad will be eating."

"Sure. I'll come over after I bring in the horses and get Amos settled for the night. Probably around eight. He usually naps on the way home from PT, but he didn't today."

"Great." She wouldn't abuse his generosity. But she was afraid to use the phone or regular mail to contact Lynn, and after all her help, her friend needed to know that she and Christie were okay and settled somewhere new.

Thoughts of Lynn brought back the reason they were running, and an involuntary chill moved through her.

"Something wrong?"

"No, not at all," she said with another quick smile. "I was just thinking it's good that you have a lot of chicken and fish in your freezer if you want to eat healthy."

Which had nothing to do with her shivering, but he didn't call her on it.

"I wike fish!"

He smiled at Christie before his gaze rebounded to Erin's. "I do, too, but we *are* going to have beef once in a while, aren't we? Maybe the occasional pork chop?"

"Of course," she laughed, "I work for you. You can have anything you like."

The flicker of desire in his eyes brought back the disturbing flush that was now becoming second nature to Erin whenever she was around him. It was a look that made her think of warm nights and soft whispers, even though daylight still shone through the window over the sink.

Looking away, she busied herself searching for more silverware beneath the bubbles. "I don't think an occasional steak or roast will do any harm."

"Good," he murmured. "I'd hate to think we were raising steers for the fun of it." He pushed away from the sink. "I'm going to catch the news with Amos. Don't dry the dishes—just leave them in the drainer. I'll put them away later."

"I can dry them. There aren't that many."

But Mac was nodding at Christie. "Leave them. Take her back to the house and get her into some dry clothes. It's after six now. Your time's your own."

"All right," she answered, realizing that Mac might want some private time with his granddad. She pulled the plug in the sink and lifted Christie down from the chairs, ignoring her flailing and whining for more play-time. "I'll just finish up and see you in the morning."

Mac's gaze fell to the front of her shirt...and clouded.

Erin looked down.

There was a wet, child-size handprint darkening the light-blue fabric of her blouse. It couldn't have been more strategically placed on Erin's left breast if she'd handed Christie a diagram. Reddening, she looked back up at Mac, who finally realized he was staring.

Clearing his throat, he turned away, echoed her "See you in the morning," then disappeared into the living room where Amos had suddenly turned up the volume on the TV set.

Erin swallowed hard as she dried the water splashes

from Amos's sturdy chairs, then returned them to the table. Because from the way Mac had stared at her, there was no mistaking the fact that, given the chance, he would have gladly made that wet mark on her breast man-size.

Chapter 3

The night air was still warm, fragrant with pine when Mac arrived at eight-thirty. Erin felt more than a little awkward when he knocked and waited to be admitted into his own home. Or maybe she was uneasy because darkness was falling, Christie was already asleep…and the last look they'd shared had been laced with tension. She mentioned her initial reservation as Mac walked inside.

His boots thudded softly as he crossed the large circular rug on the hardwood floor. "For the time being, this is your home," he answered. "I'd never invade your privacy by just walking in." He glanced around as he stepped into the office off the foyer and clicked on the small gooseneck lamp atop the computer desk. "Is Christie asleep?"

"Yes. She crashed around seven-thirty."

"How does she like her bed?"

"She loves it—but she's not in it."

"No?"

She watched him frown at the collection of boxes he'd shuttled from the spare room to this one. Then, digging in, he moved a maple chair to the computer area and began stacking the boxes in the far corner of the room. Every movement showcased the powerful flex and play of his back muscles through his white polo shirt.

Erin gave herself a mental shake and answered his question. "She has fun lining up her dollies and stuffed animals on it for their naps, but I think she feels more secure sleeping with me right now. She'll adjust. She always does."

Mac slanted her another of those critical looks, then left the pile of boxes to turn on his computer. He motioned Erin into the office chair while he pulled the spare maple one close. Tiny blips of excitement danced along her nerve endings as he dragged his chair even closer, and the shifting air carried a scent to her that was part fresh citrus and all musky man.

"It's pretty standard," he said. A dozen bright icons appeared on the monitor. "Click on the telephone icon to connect to the Internet, then when the search engine comes up, you'll see another icon on the task bar. Click on the little mailbox, and you're in." He paused. "Go ahead."

When his e-mail page came up, he reached across her, the dark hair on his forearm brushing her arm. With a few quick keystrokes, he entered his password and set the computer to remember it. Then he sank back in his chair. "Okay, my password's saved, now you can use it whenever you want. All I ask is that you use the start button to park it before you shut it off."

"I will. That's the way my laptop's set up, too. Thank you."

"You're welcome. Do you want to post a message now?"

She shook her head. No, she wanted to write to Lynn, but she didn't want him anywhere in the vicinity when she did it. She needed privacy when she contacted people from her past. She was fairly certain she could contact Lynn safely using Mac's e-mail address. "If it's okay with you, I'll do it later."

"Sure." With a few more keystrokes, he shut it down, then turned to her as if to say something more. Erin felt her pulse quicken as their gazes locked and the temperature in the small, intimately lit room inched up several degrees.

Abruptly she pushed to her feet. This was ridiculous. She wasn't sure what was going through his mind, but she knew what was happening in hers, and it was dangerous to remain sitting here. But while putting some distance between them was the best solution, she couldn't ask him to leave his own home. "I made a cinnamon coffee cake earlier if you'd like to have a slice." At least that would move them to the kitchen table where the lights were brighter, and they'd be sitting a respectable distance from each other.

The look in Mac's dark eyes told her that he'd sensed the change in temperature, too. "Coffee cake?" he repeated, slowly coming to his feet, too, and towering over her.

She nodded. "My thank-yous were getting repetitive, so I thought I'd express my gratitude with food. There's fresh decaf to go with it. If you want."

Abruptly, Erin shook her head in frustration. "I'm sorry. I'm not doing this very well. I seem to be playing hostess, but this is your home and I—'' She pressed a finger to her lips, then removed it. ''I'm just not sure what the protocol is at this point.''

''I've already told you, for now, it's your home. Tell you what. If you'll stop feeling uncomfortable about living here, I won't feel uncomfortable if I have to get something from my rooms or check my own e-mail.'' He smiled a little as he headed for the door. ''As for the coffee cake, I know I'll be sorry, but I have to pass. As I said earlier, I don't like leaving Amos unattended for long periods of time. My not being here this morning when you arrived was a fluke. I got a call and had to take care of something at the store.''

''Of course,'' she murmured, following and still embarrassed, hoping he didn't think she'd been offering more than cake. ''I'll bring it to the house tomorrow morning and you can both enjoy it.''

''Sounds good,'' he said, stepping out on the porch. ''Thanks.''

It was fully dark now, a few stars and a sliver of moon shining through the thick pines, but light from inside spilled through the windows. Mac paused beside the door, his expression troubled.

''There was something else I wanted to talk to you about tonight. Amos's PT.''

Concerned, Erin stepped out on the porch, too. ''I asked him how it went, and he said it was fine—that he's getting stronger every day.''

A skeptical tone entered his voice. ''He also told you that we fired the first housekeeper because she was interested in more than doing laundry and baking cookies.''

''And you said that wasn't true. Why *was* she let go?''

He considered the question for a long moment before he answered. "One night Amos had to use the bathroom during the wee hours, and she made him feel ashamed for needing her help. Sometimes it takes him a while to get his bad leg moving—it stiffens on him. He was depressed for days afterward because he couldn't handle a simple thing like using the toilet on his own."

Erin felt a rush of sympathy. "Oh, Mac, how awful for him."

"Yeah. It meant a lot when you said you wouldn't have a problem with that sort of thing."

It had? At the time, he'd barely acknowledged her statement. "What *about* his physical therapy? *Isn't* it going well?"

"It is, and it isn't. He's getting better—and he wants to get better. But he's not doing the exercises Vicki gives him as often as he should. It's slowing his recovery."

"How can I help?"

Mac released a burdened breath. "I can't tell you how much I hoped you'd say that. The exercises she gives him can easily be done while he's lying on his bed or sitting watching TV—exercises to strengthen his leg. Having said that, he's also getting too fond of his recliner. We need to get him up and moving."

"Then that's what we'll do," she replied decisively.

He wasn't convinced. "It won't be easy. He's a world-class crab when he's forced to do anything. He climbs all over me when I suggest it."

"Then Christie and I will make it so much fun, he won't mind."

Mac cocked his head, obviously amused. "Forgive me, but how do you propose to do that?"

Erin smiled, feeling a sudden kinship with the tall man looming over her. Dealing with Amos would be like dealing with Christie. She couldn't count the number of times she'd had to improvise to get some co-operation from her. "I don't know yet. This is still new territory. But we'll think of something."

"Understand, I'm not asking for miracles—and of course, we'll increase your pay."

"Don't do that. Helping him exercise will make me feel a little less like I'm taking advantage of your hospitality. Believe me, I'm getting a lot more out of this arrangement than you are."

"No more than anyone else we would have hired."

That wasn't so, but she could hardly explain. She didn't know him well enough to explain. She would *never* know him well enough. Suddenly that made her a little sad.

"You know," he murmured, "I had my doubts about you when I saw how young you were. I wanted someone older. Someone we knew." The night song of the crickets played in the darkness, wrapping them in another kind of intimacy, an intimacy that was somehow more potent. "I figured you'd be just one more woman who needed a job and phoned it in."

"I'd never do that."

He nodded as though he knew that now. Then he paused, reached out…and stroked her face.

Erin stood breathlessly as his index finger trailed down the slope of her cheek to her chin. It was the gentlest of touches. It was no more than a whisper against her skin, and it was hypnotic because she'd never been touched so tenderly before. Her nerve endings thrummed as he tipped her face up to his.

"You honestly care about people, don't you?"

"I try," she whispered, knowing this was inappropriate, yet unwilling to stop it. He was good and decent and so toe-curlingly sexy and attractive...and it had been so long since a man had shown any interest in her as a woman. So long since she'd *wanted* any man to show interest.

Mac's head dipped slowly and surely toward hers, his voice taking on a husky rasp, his warm breath bathing her lips. "You can't imagine how refreshing that is, Terri."

The crash of a thousand cymbals couldn't have jolted her more.

Erin backpedaled away, her pulse and heartbeat banging triple time. She wanted to say something, but suddenly, didn't know what it was. *Was* there a correct thing to say at a time like this? Apparently not, because her lips weren't moving and not a sound was coming from her throat.

Mac swore beneath his breath and expelled a ragged blast of air. "Well," he said with obvious self-loathing, "that wasn't the brightest thing I've ever done. I'm sorry. I don't know what I was thinking."

She did. It was the same thing she'd been thinking. "There's no need to apologize," she managed, working to bring her popping nerve endings under control. "Nothing happened."

"No?"

Yes, it had. But confessing that she'd wanted that kiss, too, was begging for trouble. Worse, if he hadn't called her Terri just then, she might have let him do a whole lot more—and that was a staggering realization for a woman who'd come to dread sexual contact.

"Okay," she amended, "gratitude happened. You needed to talk about your granddad's illness, and I was a convenient sounding board who said what you needed to hear. Don't worry about it.'' Her voice was stronger now, but a jittery warmth still pinged through her bloodstream. "Good night. And thanks again for letting me use your computer. I promise not to blow it up.''

The moon was a faint light, but she could still see relief in his eyes, hear it in his voice. "If you blow it up, we'll get it fixed. See you in the morning.''

"We'll be there at eight.''

Mac stalked back to the house, thoroughly fed up with himself. Good God, where was his mind? She was Amos's housekeeper, not a woman they'd brought in for his use! He checked on Amos, then strode down the sloping hill to the barn, his nerve endings still bouncing around like jumping beans. He'd groom Pike. He needed to do something to work off his tension, and cold showers sure as hell didn't turn him on—or off.

Clicking on the light in the tack room, he grabbed a brush and currycomb, and a moment later was murmuring to the horse and taking the comb through Pike's tangled mane. The gelding bumped a nose at him—probably to tell him it was almost nine-thirty, and the rest of High Hawk had retired to their TV sets or beds by now.

"Yeah, I know,'' Mac grumbled, stroking the chestnut's white blaze. "But I won't be hitting the hay anytime soon. Mind keeping me company for a while?'' The horse nosed into his hand again. "Good. Then let's get you spruced up. It's been a while, hasn't it?''

Unfortunately, as he combed and smoothed, his thoughts were elsewhere. He couldn't get those dark-blue eyes out of his mind, or that hair she insisted on tying back tight to her head. It was beautiful hair…hair that should be hanging loose around her face. Hair that would feel like silk against a man's chest.

He scowled as his libido got squarely behind that thought and started a new response south of his belt buckle. He hadn't felt a gut-gnawing attraction like this since Audra. Half of the free world knew what a colossal mistake that had been. But early on, he'd been so blinded by her wide smiles and teasing eyes that he couldn't see how different they were. Way too different for the ''opposites attract'' thing to work. And who in hell ever decided that having absolutely nothing in common was a sure path to falling in love and staying there?

But he *had* loved her. Deeply. Madly. Stupidly.

Pike shifted and stomped in his stall, and Mac realized the grooming process had gotten more energetic than he'd intended. ''Sorry, boy,'' he muttered. ''It'll be just another minute, then I'll go bug Gypsy and Jett, and let you get some shut-eye. One of us should sleep tonight.'' And he doubted it'd be him.

A half hour later Mac trudged up the stairs to his room, grabbed a pair of running shorts, then retraced his steps. He'd shower in the new bathroom, the one off the laundry room he'd had installed while Amos was in rehab. The upstairs pipes rattled, and he didn't want to wake Amos.

Only the glow from a night-light shone through the partially open doorway. Mac entered, flicked on the overhead light…and stared.

He would never get used to seeing the grab bars and supports around the tub and toilet, or the long bar against the wall. Ditto the shower curtain, which provided easy access instead of the glass doors Mac had originally suggested. For some reason, tonight it all made him feel lousier than usual.

Stripping, feeling his mood plummet, he turned on the water, waited a few seconds, then stepped inside.

Dammit, the strong man who'd raised him was getting old. Amos, who'd taught him to ride bareback and shown him how to topple paper-cup pyramids by flicking rubber bands off his fingertip.

Amos, who'd once hoisted eighty-pound feed bags with ease and now sometimes needed help getting to the bathroom.

Mac's throat tightened as he scrubbed the soap over his chest and arms, lathering away the smell of horse-flesh, seeing his granddad as he was the day he opened his door and his arms to his daughter's ten-year-old son. Except for college and four years in New Hampshire's White Mountains, he'd been with Amos for twenty-five years. *Twenty-five years!* And his grandfather had always been as strong as an ox.

Or maybe he hadn't wanted to see the telltale signs of aging as the years passed, or face his granddad's mortality. Amos was all he had in the way of family, other than an aunt, uncle and a couple of cousins in Texas.

Shelving the soap, Mac braced his hands against the front wall and let the heavy spray beat his hair down to his brows. Let it beat his shoulders and back.

There was nothing like a healthy dose of reality to ground a man. Suddenly his need to jump Terri Fletcher's pretty bones wasn't nearly as important as it was a while ago.

Wednesday and Thursday were busy but mostly satisfying, Erin decided, because Mac made himself scarce, arriving home only an hour before she took Christie back to their quarters. He didn't exactly ignore her, but he was distant—cordial in a stranger-to-stranger way as he discussed various local topics during dinner. His reserve didn't include Christie, however, and he joked and played with her until she giggled uncontrollably, warming to him in a way she'd never done with Charles. And that was fine with Erin. They needed to keep their distance now that they both recognized the attraction simmering beneath their socially correct behavior.

On Friday afternoon a violent storm came out of nowhere.

"Just open them doors and move outta the way, pronto!" Amos shouted to her from the porch. "They'll come in fast!"

"I will!" she yelled back over the howling wind and rain. Erin pulled Amos's hooded poncho more tightly around herself and ran toward the barn, rubberized canvass flapping. The rain was coming down in sheets.

She'd been aware of the rain, but she hadn't known it was a problem until thunder jolted Amos from his post-PT nap, and he'd sat bolt upright, insisting he had to get the horses back in the barn. "Lightning spooks 'em so bad, they'll beat down the fences!" he'd persisted. But no way could he manage the task, so that left Erin to manage the situation. Thankfully, Christie was still napping.

A new bolt of lightning ripped and crackled through the dark thunderheads, and the earth trembled. Erin ran faster, seeing the horses now. Grouped together at the far side of the long corral, they skittered anxiously, ran in circles—whinnied and tossed their big heads.

Yanking open the barn door, she hurried inside and passed the stalls, blinking and wiping the rain from her face as her eyes adjusted to the dim light. It was only a little after four o'clock, but the weather and dense cloud cover made it look more like eight.

Striding up an aisle lined with hay bales, she spied the wide doors that opened onto the corral and rushed toward them. Lightning flashed again and lit up the barn. Fumbling with the latch, Erin threw open the double doors to the raging wind and rain, then blanched as the horses picked up the movement and, wheeling, thundered directly for her.

Heart slamming into her throat, she hugged the wall, afraid to breathe as they ran inside, the darker horse nearly losing its footing on the wet straw. Then, just as Amos said they would, they slowed, calmed and found their respective stalls.

Bracing herself, she hurried into the rain again to snatch the door rings, lost her hood in the wind, then yanked the double doors shut and relatched them. Rain still punished the shingled roof, but with the doors closed, the barn was a little quieter now.

Relieved that she hadn't been trampled, Erin turned around.

Adrenaline jolted her as her unsuspecting gaze collided with Mac's. His hair was plastered to his forehead, and rain streamed down his face and dripped off his chin to his soaked shirt.

"You're drenched," he growled, reaching overhead to click on a bare-bulb light. He whisked the rain from his face. "What in hell are you doing down here?"

She shot him an affronted look. What did he think

she was doing down here? "The storm was spooking your horses. The only way I could keep your grandfather from bringing them inside—rather, attempting to bring them inside—was to do it myself."

Mac swore, exasperated. "Where's Christie?"

"At the house. She's asleep on the sofa." Erin reached beneath the poncho and plucked her baby monitor from her waistband. Toddler snores flowed from it, though they were almost drowned out by the pouring rain and the low sound of Amos's TV program.

Then suddenly what he'd said and the critical tone he'd used pushed her annoyance to anger. "Did you think I'd leave her wandering the house alone with a man who's recovering from a stroke? How nice. You barely speak directly to me in two days, and when you finally do, you practically accuse me of negligence." She pushed past him. "I have to get back to her."

"Terri, wait." Mac grabbed her hand. "I didn't mean anything by that. I was just concerned. And Amos should have realized that I'd come home and take care of the horses when I saw that a storm was brewing. They would've been okay until I got here."

"He was sure they'd break through the fence or hurt themselves."

"They would have been fine," Mac repeated.

Erin took a few seconds to compose herself, then nodded. "All right. I'll know that next time. And I'm sorry I overreacted about Christie, but I'd *never* put her at risk. She's my whole life. Now I have to go. I don't want her to wake up, be afraid of the storm and find me gone."

"I'll drive you. The truck's right outside."

"What about the horses? Shouldn't you—"

"I'll get some of the water off them after I take you back." She felt another jolt when he reached behind her neck to pull Amos's floppy hood up over her wet hair. "We'll pick up Christie, then I'll take you both down to the house so you can change. You're soaked to the skin."

"That's okay. I haven't started dinner yet."

"We'll order takeout."

"Mac, I have chicken thawing."

"It'll keep." With a hand on her back, he guided her to the open doors at the front of the barn. Rain was still coming down, and thunder rumbled overhead.

Something must have struck him funny then, because the skin beside his dark eyes crinkled and he started to laugh.

"What's so entertaining?" she asked, thinking about being annoyed again.

Mac fingered her dripping hood and the long wet bangs that stuck to her forehead and sides of her face. "I was just thinking that you've done enough today. If you did any more, we'd have to give you hazard pay."

Grinning, he gestured through the pounding rain to the truck he'd parked close to the doors. "Okay. Run for it, Terri Fletcher." And suddenly she was grinning, too.

They had to run again when they got to the house, though Mac took the truck as close as he could to the porch steps. Amos was there to scold them when they entered, wiping their faces and laughing.

"Are the two of you daft?" he asked crossly, though there was a hint of humor in his eyes. "Never saw two people more happy to be wet."

"Never had so much fun *getting* wet," Mac returned, and smiled at Erin. And against every warning bell clanging in her mind, her heart grew wings.

The mood was still light when he drove Erin and Christie back to their quarters after an early dinner of delivery pizza, tossed salads and fresh apple cobbler. She'd dug in her heels and insisted she didn't need to change to dry clothes—and eventually Mac had conceded. Besides, she'd pointed out to him, someone had to stay with Amos while he tended the horses. Erin knew it was wrong to feel this content, but she couldn't stop herself from embracing it. It had been years since she'd laughed over something silly.

"You're a good cook," he said, carrying Christie over the wet grass and up the steps to the house. The heavy rain had stopped, and a smudge of sunlight shone faintly through the thinning cloud cover. He held the door for Erin, then he and Christie followed her inside.

"Thanks. Of course, the most difficult dish was the pizza."

"And it was excellent." Mac nodded toward his computer room. "Mind if I pick up my e-mail messages before I head back?"

Feeling a guilty twinge, she said, "Of course not." Then more casually she added, "I need to get Christie in the tub and ready for bed, so take all the time you want."

As the two of them headed for the bathroom, Mac lingered in the doorway, listening.

"Hey, sweetie pie," Erin murmured. "How would you like a bubble bath tonight?"

"Waggedy Ann, too?"

"Nope. Sorry. Raggedy Ann would take forever to

dry, and she likes to sleep with you. You don't want to sleep in a wet bed, do you?''

He didn't hear Christie's reply because they'd gone into the bathroom, but he assumed she'd said no.

Mac pushed away from the doorframe and went to his desk, then started his PC. He paused to listen again as the rush of running water and giggles echoed from the bathroom. On the heels of that, the smell of shampoo and bubble bath carried to him. They were nice sounds. Nice smells. A reminder of a life he'd once looked forward to having. But Audra had changed that.

A nerve leaped in his jaw as he indulged in a little leftover resentment. Then he reminded himself that that part of his life had been over for a long time, and concentrated on his e-mail. There were four messages, one of them from his New Hampshire friend, Shane Garrett, who was just touching base. He answered Shane's note first, then moved on to the others.

He hadn't realized how much time he'd spent until Terri walked in, holding Christie's hand.

The sight of the little girl's rosy cheeks and damp, baby-fine hair curling at the ends brought a smile to his face. ''Don't you look pretty,'' he said.

''I taked a bubbo baff!''

''You *took* a bubble bath,'' Terri said. ''And now it's time for bed. Can you say good-night to Mr. Corbett?''

'''Night, Misser Corvet.''

''Sweet dreams, honey,'' Mac answered.

When Terri returned a few minutes later, all thoughts of Christie vanished. She'd gotten rid of that rubber-band-thing strangling her hair, and now it curved softly over her forehead and brushed her high cheekbones, then fell to her shoulders.

He tore his gaze away, beginning to hear jungle drums pounding in his head, beginning to feel the heat. "There were no e-mail messages for you. I recognized all the senders. You might want to tell your friends to put your name in the subject line so I don't open any of your mail by mistake."

"That's a good idea. I haven't written to anyone yet, but I'll probably do that soon. Thanks again for letting me use your e-mail address."

"Sure." He paused for a beat. He didn't want to leave, but there was no offer of coffee tonight. Besides, he had to get back to Amos. Mac ambled to the door, rested a hand on the doorknob. "With the rain and all, I didn't ask how PT went today."

"It went really well, I think. Vicki asked me to come in and watch, so I saw the exercises your granddad is supposed to do—especially on the days he doesn't have a session. And guess what? He did a few of them when he came home."

Mac feigned shock. "You're kidding. Without being badgered?"

"Completely on his own. I'm not sure, but I think— and I could be wrong about this—that he wants to please me. I caught him glancing in my direction occasionally when he was doing his leg lifts. I told him if he kept that up, I'd be looking for another job sooner than I'd planned. He seemed to like that."

Mac felt a swell of gratitude…and something else he didn't care to name. In just five short days—without even trying, it seemed—she'd found a place in Amos's heart. She and Christie both had. He smiled down at her, liking the way she smiled back. "You're a miracle worker."

"I doubt that."

''I don't,'' he murmured, and captured her hand. He held it for a long moment, giving her time to decide if she wanted it back. Then, when she didn't tug it away, he brought it slowly to his lips. Mac watched her eyes widen as he rubbed his lips over the tips of her fingers, good sense gradually losing out to the new heat stirring in his blood.

Then without really knowing how it happened, suddenly she was in his arms, his hands were sliding through all that hair, and his eager mouth was slanting over hers.

Chapter 4

Mac slid his hands over her body, deepening the kiss, molding her soft curves to his hollows and planes, hearing those drums again and letting them fill his blood, his lungs, his very soul. It had been so long since a woman had felt this good in his arms, so long since he'd *wanted*. And now he wanted with every breath in his body.

With a muffled sound, Terri jerked away.

His fevered haze cleared the instant he saw the startled look in her eyes. *Oh, hell.* Hadn't she wanted this, too? Or had his deprived libido just made some male-friendly assumptions and plunged ahead?

The awkwardness seemed to stretch out forever... until Terri backed away a few steps and filled the silence.

"I'd better check on Christie," she said quietly.

Mac released a ragged breath and nodded. Of all the things she could have said, that was probably the best.

If she wanted to pretend the kiss never happened, that was fine with him. No harm, no foul. It seemed to him that there was an unwritten code of honor that said you didn't mess with the help, and he'd nearly done it twice.

Opening the door, he stepped out on the porch and spoke through the screen. A thin, drizzling rain had begun again. "Tomorrow's Saturday so you'll have a short day. I'll be closing the store at three."

"Your...your granddad mentioned that. Would you like me to start supper?"

"Thanks, but I can do that." He considered offering an apology, but he knew he'd never be able to pull it off. He wasn't sorry. She'd tasted like every sweet thing he'd been missing in life, and his blood was still pumping in all the wrong directions. If she hadn't pulled back— Shaking off that thought, he descended the steps. "Good night, Terri."

"Good night."

Mac heard the door close behind him as he climbed inside the truck, fired the engine and flicked on the windshield wipers. Backing away from the house, he drove onto the dirt and grass lane that joined Amos's driveway to his.

Two nights ago, he'd vowed to keep his distance. Now, forty-eight hours later, he was on her like a rutting Neanderthal with bad teeth and a knobby club. *Man need jump. Get in cave.*

He bumped the truck through the ruts, grimly renewing his promise to stay away from her. Even if she wasn't an employee, from the way she'd balked when his hands slid to her hips, she wasn't the one-night-stand type. She was also an unknown commodity and liked the road too much for him to consider her anything but temporary. So logically, since there would be no sex with her without a commitment—and he wasn't interested in one—keeping his distance should be easy.

Mac pulled up to his granddad's house and stared bleakly at the low lamps burning in the windows while his pulse continued to beat to the tune of his need. Yep. Easy. Easy as walking on water.

Erin's hand shook as she turned off the light in the foyer, then watched the cherry-red taillights in Mac's truck wink out in front of Amos's house. She heard the low thud of the truck's door shutting.

Why hadn't she stopped him when she saw that kiss coming? She knew it was a mistake. Instead, she'd stilled for it, breathlessly awaited it, almost willed his warm, talented mouth onto hers. She swallowed the lump in her throat. But hadn't she deserved just one tiny moment of tenderness and touching? Just one brief moment of feeling like a woman again, not just Christie's mom or someone's employee or an habitual newcomer to a new town who was always in fear?

But instead of being tender, that very short kiss had been electric. Pulses still throbbed, from her head to her toes.

Pulling herself away, Erin walked to Mac's room where Christie lay sleeping on his giant bed, the sheet kicked off, her smooth little legs jutting out from her ruffled baby doll pajamas. Her thumb was nowhere near her mouth, and Erin breathed a thankful prayer. It had taken time and talking and tenderness, but Christie had finally given up that needed comfort a few months ago.

Erin slid the sheet over her daughter's legs and

stroked her sweet face, then quietly left the room to put the kettle on for tea.

She could still feel a tingle on her lips, still feel her nerve endings vibrate beneath her skin. But Mac was forbidden fruit. An involvement of any kind was impossible—with him or with anyone else. Despite her promise to care for Amos for the next six to eight weeks, she knew life could change in the blink of an eye. She pulled a thick mug from a cupboard. What happened in Maine could happen again. It was pointless to start something she couldn't afford to finish.

Bells pealed from the soaring spire of the tiny, nondenominational church in High Hawk on Sunday morning as Erin and Christie filed out, exchanging vague pleasantries with members of the congregation, then shaking hands and complimenting the aging minister on his service. Overhead, the sun shone brightly, and as they walked to the van with those church bells still clanging a welcome, Erin felt almost normal.

Suddenly she grinned down at Christie. "How would you like to have breakfast at a restaurant this morning, sweetheart?"

Christie's eyes sparkled. "Wif Aunt Millie?"

"No," she answered, wishing it were so. "Aunt Millie's restaurant is far away." In the five months they'd spent in Maine, Millie had become a wonderful friend and Christie's aunt-of-the-heart. Erin missed her, too, sometimes terribly, but there was nothing she could do about that. She continued speaking to Christie. "How would you like to eat at the little place with the funny stools that spin? Remember? You had French fries there when we first came here." Bending low, she added in a conspiratorial whisper, "We could have pancakes!"

That was all the temptation Christie needed.

But twenty minutes later as Christie dragged her silver-dollar pancakes through a river of syrup and Erin sipped from her coffee cup, a niggling fear crept in again and she found herself sliding veiled looks over the room, checking for men who glanced away or hid behind newspapers when she caught them looking. Maine was over two weeks behind them, and though she knew Charles would never stop searching for them, there was no good reason to think they'd been followed here. She'd lost the private investigator's dark-blue sedan just outside of Boston, and she hadn't used her credit card or done anything else that would create a paper trail. Just the same, the short hairs at the nape of her neck began to prickle, and suddenly Erin had the eerie feeling that someone was watching them.

Then she saw him. A man in a back booth, youngish, wearing a light navy windbreaker and tinted glasses. He sent her a slow smile and rose from his seat, carried his check to the front of the room.

Erin's pulse skyrocketed. Pushing aside her half-eaten English muffin, she took Christie's fork and fed her to hurry her along.

Then a waitress called him by name, asked how his sister's wedding went, and Erin's heart settled down. She had to relax. She was jumping at shadows. The man was simply one of the locals, probably curious at seeing a new face. Still, she needed to be careful. She hadn't been careful enough in Maine.

The phone rang. Mac pushed away from the table where he'd been tallying the week's receipts, then went to answer it before it woke Amos. Last time he'd checked, his granddad was snoring in his recliner, enjoying a post-supper nap, sections of the Sunday paper strewn in a half moat around his chair. Mac had gathered the papers and set them aside, irked that Amos hadn't seen them as a danger to his slipping and falling.

He snatched up the receiver before the phone could ring a second time. "Hello?"

A familiar voice returned the greeting. "Hi, Mac. I tried to get you at your place, but there was no answer, so I figured you were at your granddad's."

No one had answered his phone?

Craning his neck to see his house through the window, Mac said, "Yeah, I'm here, Shane. What's up?" He knew Terri and Christie had come home a while ago, so why wasn't she answering the phone? Then he saw them splashing at the corner of the pond, Christie in a ruffled yellow bathing suit, Terri in tan shorts and a white tank top. A little pop of adrenaline hit him.

"Just wondering if you'd given any thought to my suggestion," Shane went on.

Frowning, Mac dragged his attention away from the pond. "What suggestion?"

"Aren't you checking your e-mail?"

No, he wasn't. After that debacle on Friday night, he was staying as far away from Terri as he could. Since his computer was in his house—and so was she—no, he was not checking his email. To Shane he simply said, "Haven't checked it for a day or two."

"Oh. Well, I wrote and offered you a proposition. You might want to read it."

"What kind of proposition?"

"Good, you're eager," he said with a short laugh. "I think my note began, 'Aren't you tired of running your granddad's general store yet?' and ended with, 'I've had it with New Hampshire, and I'm coming back to Arizona to start a new business.'" He paused. "I've already looked into office space. I'm hoping you'll make it a partnership."

Mac held back a sigh. What was it people said? Timing was everything?

Shane had been a good friend for years. They'd attended Arizona State together, drank more than they should've at frat parties but still made the dean's list, hunted, fished, went white-water rafting and even dated twin sisters for a while. It had been Mac's lousy luck to *marry* his twin. After graduation, he and Shane had both snagged jobs with the same civil engineering firm in New Hampshire.

Mac had cut out and come home after his divorce, putting all of his energies into building his house. Because he knew this was where he was going to stay.

"You're not saying anything," Shane prompted. "Come on, building dams has to be a hell of a lot more fun than carrying old ladies' groceries to their cars."

Mac grinned. "They're not all old."

"No?"

"No."

Shane laughed. "Do I hear renewed interest in the fair sex? Or just a renewed interest in sex, period? Something going on that you haven't mentioned?"

Terri's face—and now her long, finally uncovered legs—filled his mind. "No, and I guess things aren't working out with Lisa if you're thinking of pulling up stakes."

"She says I need to grow up."

Mac grinned again. "She's right. Ever look up the word cavalier in the dictionary? There's a picture of you next to it."

Shane groaned. "See, that's why this partnership's so important. You used to be sharper. Wittier. Slinging feed sacks is dulling your brain. You need a challenge."

He had one, Mac thought. Five feet, six inches of her. She challenged his senses, challenged his sleep, challenged his peace of mind.

He heard Amos begin to stir, and caregiver mode clicked in. Prolonged inactivity still made Amos a little wobbly when he got up. "Shane, I have to take care of something right now, but I'll call you in a few days. I need some time to think about this."

"Just e-mail me and save yourself a dime. All I need is one word, and you know what it is."

Terri's clear complexion and thickly lashed blue eyes filled his mind again. "I'll *phone*. Have a good—"

"Wait a second," Shane cut in almost reluctantly. "There's something else. This won't take long."

Reluctance? From Shane? "What's up?"

"I ran into your ex-mother-in-law yesterday."

Dread settled between Mac's shoulder blades, but he kept his tone even. "Yeah? What did Vivian have to say?"

"Audra remarried a few months ago."

"Good for her," he said unemotionally, but he felt the old fish hook turn in his gut. "Anyone I know?"

"Yeah," Shane replied. "Yeah, you know him."

He didn't have to say more. The guy she'd married

was the slick used-car salesman she'd been sleeping with while they were together: Buzz Willett.

"Mac, she's pregnant."

His heart stopped. When it started again, every beat was a reminder of Audra's deceit. "We've been divorced for two years. She has her life, and I have mine."

"Good," his friend replied without a lot of conviction. "Glad to hear it. Just thought you should know."

Mac muttered something he hoped was appropriate in return, hating the hollow feeling in his chest after so long. He didn't love her anymore. That was something he knew without a doubt, because he could never love a woman he didn't trust. But this thing with the baby hit him in a different place. In his pride. "I'll call you about the partnership in a week or so. Right now things are too up in the air to make plans. But thanks for asking."

"Just call me back with the right answer."

Mac said goodbye and hung up. So Audra had married the creep. Well, bon voyage and have a happy life.

Still bitter? a small voice asked.

Damn right he was bitter. Learning that she'd been screwing around on him had been bad enough. Finding out that *he'd* been paying for Buzz and Audra's motel rooms and fancy dinners, courtesy of their joint savings account had really knocked him on his ass. Then, the coup de grâce. While he'd been waiting from month to month to see if she was pregnant, she'd been swallowing birth control pills and making sure it wouldn't happen. Having his baby wasn't on her agenda.

Having Buzz Willett's kid was.

"Who was that on the phone?" Amos called from the living room.

"Nobody," Mac returned.

"Didn't sound like nobody."

A nerve leaped in Mac's jaw. "It was Shane, Granddad. He just called to touch base."

"Then why did you say it was nobody? Somethin' goin' on you don't want me to know about?"

Muttering a breathy curse, he walked into the living room, his lousy mood following like a stray dog. "No, there's nothing going on, and I don't know why I said it was nobody. Do you need anything from the kitchen? Something to drink? Or do you want to get up and walk around a little?"

Amos looked up at him in annoyance. "No, I want to sit right here and finish readin' the paper. If I get thirsty, I'll get my own drink. You don't have t' wait on me."

"Then maybe *I'll* take a walk. I've been staring at the books too long." He needed some time alone, without questions being fired at him every two seconds.

"Go," Amos said, sliding his reading glasses down from where they stuck to his forehead.

"All right. I won't be long."

Mac filled his lungs with the fresh pine air and sunshine as he descended the porch steps and started toward the pasture where the horses grazed alongside Amos's red-coated Herefords. Then he saw Terri and Christie, still laughing and splashing in the pond and his plans changed. Suddenly his boots were moving toward Terri. They hadn't spoken much since that ill-advised kiss Friday night. Hopefully, enough time had elapsed for them to get back on a decent footing. He needed a distraction. He needed to think about something besides Audra's pregnancy. And why *his* child wouldn't have been welcomed.

"Hi, cutie," he said to Christie when he'd hunkered down beside them on the grassy bank. "I didn't know you could swim."

Christie flapped her arms, showing off the inflated yellow cuffs above her elbows. "Mommy buyed me water wings!" Her excitement ebbed. "But you can't fwy wif 'em."

"You can't?"

Christie shook her head.

"Well, they look like fun, anyway." He worked up a passable smile for Terri. Even with her hair knotted at the nape of her neck and strands from those too-long bangs falling into her eyes, she was beautiful. Lousy as he felt, he still took in her long, shapely legs, starting at the cuff of her tan shorts and ending with her polished-pink toenails flashing beneath the water. "Glad you're enjoying the pond."

She tugged her wet cuffs lower on her thighs. "I checked with your grandfather a few days ago," she said, her gaze increasingly curious as it moved over his face. "He said this end is fairly shallow, but I'm keeping Christie close, anyway."

"Probably a good idea." He glanced at Christie again. She was shoveling tiny yellow ducks into a sand pail already filled with naked Barbie dolls, then dumping them out and snatching them back before they could float away.

"How far out before it gets deep?" Terri asked.

"About twelve feet. Then it tapers from three feet to six—maybe seven—at its deepest. Amos had it put in when I was a kid. Made me a pretty popular guy."

"I imagine so. I guess you spent a lot of time here."

"Actually, I lived here," he returned, glad they were talking with some degree of comfort. He reached into the water for a blue plastic cup that had sunk to the gravel bottom, then set it aside. "My parents died in a small plane crash when I was ten. Amos took me in."

Sympathy—but not pity, he noted—flickered through her eyes. "I'm sorry. That must have been hard."

He sent her a brief, wry smile. "It wasn't easy. I'll never stop missing them, but...Amos was there for me."

"No brothers or sisters?"

"Nope." Frowning, he shifted the subject, partly because he was already tired of talking about himself, and partly because he still knew very little about her. "How about you? Are your parents still living?"

Her gaze clouded slightly. "My mom passed away five years ago, but my dad's still around. Somewhere," she added with a mirthless laugh. "They divorced when I was in high school. I haven't seen or heard from him since her funeral."

"Then, he's never met his granddaughter?"

"No. Last I heard he was living in San Diego, and—" She halted abruptly, a startled look passing over her pretty features. Then she flashed a tight smile and rose. "Time to get out, Christie."

"You don't talk much about yourself," Mac observed.

She shrugged and picked up the white towel beside her. "Be thankful. It's all boring. As for my dad, I'll probably look him up one of these days—see if there's anything between us. California's right next door."

She reached for Christie's hand and repeated, "Come on, sweetie. Time for your Barbies and ducks to dry off."

"No! I need to fwim!"

"Yes. You're starting to prune."

Christie let out a squeal as Terri lifted her out of the water and onto the bank, then promptly dissolved into tears.

"Shhh," Terri said. "You'll scare the birdies." She slipped off Christie's water wings and blotted her hair, then draped the towel over her shoulders. "You can swim some more in the tub. Now stand here like a good girl while I gather your toys."

In a flash Christie was out of the towel, her little legs pumping away from her mother. Before Mac knew it, she'd smacked into him and latched onto his thigh. "I wike it outside!"

"Christie Lynn," Terri warned. Frowning, she walked to Mac and crouched to unhook her daughter's arms from his thigh, her fingers burning through worn denim. "That's enough, now. We have to go in." But Christie hung on, Terri's hands crept higher in their struggle, and Mac felt a jolt of desire so powerful— and given the day, so unexpected—that his breath caught.

Simultaneously lifting Christie onto one of his arms and taking Terri's hand, he tugged her to her feet. "Know what?" he said to Christie. "I have an idea that's more fun than swimming."

Christie's chin quivered. "What?"

"Ice cream. There's some in my freezer. I have chocolate syrup, too." He glanced at Terri, hoping Christie's dangling legs and feet covered his indiscretion. "That is, if it's okay with Mommy." She looked irritated that he'd taken over, but he hadn't had a lot of options. Mac lowered his voice. ''Sorry if I overstepped.''

''It's okay,'' she said, then her gaze flicked back to Christie. ''Let's get a bath first—without any more crying—then we'll talk about ice cream. Okay?''

Sniffing, nodding, she reached out for her mother, and Mac let her go.

''That's my girl,'' Terri murmured, tucking the towel around her and kissing her cheek. Her shoulders sagged in dismay as she took in the front of Mac's shirt. ''I'm sorry. Now you're all wet.''

His shirt was the least of his problems. ''I'll dry.'' He bent to gather the toys, loaded them into her pail, then handed it to Christie. ''Here you go. Enjoy your treat. Ice cream's in the freezer in the basement,'' he added, meeting Terri's eyes. ''Syrup's on a shelf in the door of the refrigerator.''

''You're more than welcome to join us.''

''Nah, you two deserve a full day together. We take up too much of your time as it is.''

A troubled look entered her blue eyes. ''Christie and I have plenty of time to be together. I wish you'd reconsider. When you walked down here a few minutes ago, you looked like…well, like the day had beaten you down a little. And it *is* your ice cream and your house.'' She smiled. ''Maybe Amos would like to have a sundae, too, after all the angel food cake and fat-free whipped topping I've been pushing this week.''

Mac glanced toward Amos's white clapboard. He didn't need the stimulation of her, but the distraction and company were doing him nothing but good. ''All right,'' he finally said, bringing his gaze back to her.

"Thank you. Let me see if Amos is interested, and I'll let you know."

She smiled again. "Good. Just give me a few minutes to get Christie in and out of the tub."

The only thing Amos was interested in was an old John Wayne movie. "You go ahead," he said, his eyes glued to the TV. "I'll be fine. Already got myself a drink."

"Care if I take that can of whipped cream in the refrigerator down to the house with me? Christie might like that."

"Hell, take it all. There's cherries and caramel topping someplace under the cupboard, too. Lord knows I won't be eatin' it with that gal houndin' me day and night about my blood pressure and cholesterol."

Mac had to smile. His granddad didn't mean a word of it, and Mac knew it. "Unhappy with Terri?"

"Nah, she's okay. And even when she cooks healthy, her food's a damn sight better'n anything you fix, so I should prob'ly count my blessings. You have a good time."

Making ice cream sundaes with Christie and Terri didn't turn out to be the wholesome thing Mac had expected. Because as he watched Terri drizzle chocolate syrup over their vanilla-bean ice cream, snozzle on whipped cream and balance maraschino cherries on top of it all, Mac's mind crept happily into X-rated territory. Within minutes he had to excuse himself to check on Amos from the intercom in the great room.

"I'm watchin' the Duke," Amos yelled back over the blare of gunfire and pounding hooves. "If I need ya, I know where to find ya. Can't you find somethin' t' do?"

Mac sighed at the ceiling. He'd love to find something to do. But he doubted that he and Amos were on the same page as to what that something was, and he doubted Terri would be a willing participant with a small child in the house.

But when he returned to the kitchen and discovered the cherry on top of his sundae missing—and saw Christie's impish look—the feelings he'd been fighting ebbed a little.

He winked at Terri, then looked at Christie again. "You know, there was a cherry on my ice cream when I left the room. Who do you think took it?"

"Maybe Waggedy Ann?"

"Maybe Raggedy Ann's best friend," he said. Then he sat, glanced around at his kitchen table, so full of life and fun... and dug into his sundae.

Later, Mac lay in bed, staring through the guest room's window at the stars peeking out of the thin, tattered clouds, reflecting on Audra's carrying another man's child, and wishing he'd been thinking with his head when he'd asked her to marry him. He would've saved himself three years of lies and two years of grieving over them. Funny, though. After the initial shock of hearing about her remarriage and pregnancy, things were settling into place in his mind and he was beginning to accept that they were never meant to be together. She'd valued monetary things, had never understood the simple beauty of a crystal-clear stream or the tall, straight trunk of a Ponderosa pine. Worse, she'd seen Amos as an obligation, not a friend and family member. But Audra was the past.

Tonight all he wanted was warm, sweet, leggy Terri Fletcher. And he wanted her with a ferocity that made sleep impossible.

Chapter 5

Charles glared down from the glass wall in his office to the bustling city beneath him, impatiently clicking the tip of his pen in and out.

Late-day commuters snagged taxis while other Chicagoans moved about like wind-up toys, scurrying in and out of shops and buildings. He snapped back his left cuff and glared at his gold timepiece again, the pounding in his head worsening. Seven forty-eight. Forty-eight minutes past time, and still no word from Smith. Click, click. Click, click. Click, click.

He felt his control spiraling away, sailing out of reach.

Whirling from the glass, he hit a wall switch, and the heavy damask drapes whooshed closed behind him as he stalked to the recessed aquarium in the paneled north wall.

Inhaling and exhaling slow, metered breaths, he stared into the tank, willed himself *in there* with his neons and mollies…cerebrally joined his angel fish as they skimmed languidly through aerated water, their delicate dorsal and side fins gently undulating like the diaphanous wings of their namesakes. There were six among the coral and castles, all treasured, all hypnotic, all infinitely better at soothing his anger than Dr. Hastings Sherwood.

When the call came seventeen minutes later, most of the pounding in Charles's head had subsided. His tone was still curt as he depressed the button on the speakerphone. "You're late." Once again there was no one to hear him. The office was empty, though cleaning crews were working on the lower floors.

"I was having dinner—though I guess they call it supper here."

"Where is *here?*"

"Care to know who joined me?"

Charles paced the floor. "I repeat, *where are you?*"

"Maine. By the way, her name's Trisha, and she's very pretty, very gullible and very hot for me."

"Goddammit, punch notches in your belt on your own time. Just tell me about my wife." And she would always *be* his wife. Marriage vows were a sacred commitment. *What God has joined together, let no man put asunder.*

Smith's indifferent voice flowed from the speaker. "Don't worry, young and jiggly isn't my type. We did have some fun yesterday and again today before she started her shift at a little place called Krafty Millie's Café. Ring any bells?"

Charles's blood leaped. "This girl knows where Erin is?"

"No, but she knows where she was two days after your private investigator flashed photographs of her and your daughter around town—to the wrong people, I might add. Apparently a shopkeeper near the docks had taken a liking to your wife, and when the P.I. started asking questions, this guy phoned the café to warn her.''

This guy? A cold trembling began in Charles's gut. Click, click. Click, click. Click, click. ''Was she sleeping with him?''

''That's doubtful. Trisha said she never dated—spent all of her time with the little girl. Anyway, your family was packed and gone thirty minutes after the guy called. I'm amazed that your P.I. picked up her trail at all.''

''Where is she now?''

Smith took a drink of something and swallowed.

The pounding in Charles's head threatened to return.

''According to Trisha, Mrs. Kraft sent your wife to her brother's car dealership near Bangor. She dumped her white Ford Windstar and bought another van—different color and make.''

She'd lost his P.I. in Boston, then returned to Maine? ''Erin has contacted this girl?''

''No. The day Kraft's brother phoned the café, Trisha took the message. He told her that he'd set your ex up with a new vehicle, and to pass the information on to his sister. Mrs. Fallon is now driving a gray, 1995 Dodge Caravan with Maine plates.''

''Then she's still in Maine?''

''I don't know. Maybe. The best hiding place is one that's already been searched, right? I'll talk to you soon.''

''Wait!'' Charles shouted, feeling his control begin to slip again. ''How will you track her?''

''Let me worry about that,'' Smith replied. ''I don't

intend to canvass the highways. There are more efficient ways to find someone who doesn't want to be found.''

''Don't get too visible,'' Charles warned coldly. ''This girl, this Trisha—''

''—won't say a word. I guarantee it.''

Smith hung up.

Incensed, Charles glared at the phone, his head threatening to split in two. *He'd been dismissed?*

Punching the disconnect button, he whirled and fired his pen against the tank. Startled fish darted away. He didn't put up with insolence! Especially from employees! For $60,000 and expenses he deserved respect!

But a few minutes later as he smoothed manicured fingertips over the cool glass of the tank, he smiled at his gaily painted angels in their softly lit world. Perhaps a little insolence could be tolerated if Smith got the job done.

His passport was ready, as was Christiana's, though hers had been prepared by a talented man Charles had come to know.

The instant Smith completed his assignment, Charles would collect his daughter, and they would fly to a country without an extradition treaty with the United States. A country that respected a man's ordinance over his family. There he would raise his mother's namesake to be a proper young lady, not the duplicitous liar her mother had been.

Charles left the tank, picked up his briefcase then exited his posh office and took the elevator to the ground floor.

He had money, power and the will to succeed. That was all any man needed to get what he wanted.

Dusk gathered in the shadows of the pines and pressed against Amos's old windows. Erin clicked on the light over the sink to rinse Christie's cereal bowl and milk cup, her snack before bedtime. She was already asleep on Amos's couch, hopefully dreaming of glass slippers and fairy godmothers after story time. Amos, too, had turned in for the night after an exhausting, late-day physical therapy session.

Erin heard the low hum of Mac's burgundy Cherokee arriving, then the crunch of gravel as the vehicle came to a stop at the end of the driveway beside the house. Memories of his kiss a full week ago and their tension-laced Sunday-evening ice cream party made her pulse race and her blood warm. He'd been great that night with Christie, teasing and joking. But the attraction he'd tried to hide when their gazes collided was easy to see.

With each passing day the chemistry between them was becoming a near-tangible thing, and while she gloried in the knowledge that she *could* find a man sexually attractive again, this was the wrong time, and Mac was the wrong man.

She was drying her hands on a tea towel when he walked inside.

His brisk bootfalls quickly softened when he realized the only sound in the house was the low murmur of the all-news station. "Where's Amos?"

Erin slid the towel back through the refrigerator's long handle. "Tucked in for the night."

"Already? It's barely eight o'clock."

"He didn't nap after PT, then after supper he and Christie played Lucky Ducks and Candy Land until they were both worn out. She crashed about a half hour after he did." Erin studied his rugged features as he hung his black Stetson on a peg by the door, then braced a hand on a maple chair and tugged off his boots. "You look tired, too," she said. He also looked sexy and earthy and far too appealing with his hair falling over his brow and his strong jaw shaded.

"It's been a long day. I'll perk up after I grab a shower." It had been cool when he left early this morning to do the quarterly inventory, which was why Erin had driven Amos to PT again. Now he shrugged off the flannel shirt he wore open over his white T-shirt.

He glanced at her. "You've been up since 6 a.m., too. Why don't you look tired?"

She grinned. "Probably because women are a lot more resilient than men are. Are you hungry? I can warm the chicken and dumplings we had for supper."

Mac arched a brow as he carried his shirt past her on his way up the stairs. "Chicken and dumplings? You made gravy?"

"Chocolate cake, too—a low fat recipe. It was better than handling the mutiny that was brewing. Your granddad said he was tired of eating like a rabbit, and he wanted some decent food tonight."

Mac halted midway up the stairs, his brow lining. "Was he rude to you?"

"Not at all," she said, smiling. "He grumbled a bit, but it was good-natured grumbling. He likes me. He wouldn't be rude."

"Imagine that," Mac returned, smiling back. "A man actually liking someone like you, who's so hard to take."

A shiver ran through her because she recognized the compliment. "Imagine that."

He stared at her for another long beat, unreadable thoughts flickering through his dark gaze. Then he slowly descended the steps, reached to his right for the switch beside the staircase, and flooded the dusky kitchen with light. He started up the stairs again. "Back in a minute."

Erin stepped into the stairwell. "Mac? You didn't say if you wanted me to heat supper."

"Thanks, but I grabbed a sandwich earlier. The chocolate cake sounds good, though." He teased from the top of the steps, "I've been eating like a rabbit for the past two weeks, too."

Erin rolled her eyes. "You're not that deprived. I found a candy bar wrapper in the pocket of your jeans when I did the laundry this morning."

Her only answer was a long, low chuckle as he disappeared into the hallway.

Erin went to the cupboard to pull out a plate, her heart too warm, too happy and beating too rapidly. They'd become friends, not just allies in Amos's health care. That was a good thing. Wasn't it?

When Mac returned ten minutes later wearing clean jeans and a black polo shirt, his hair was wet and combed straight back, showing to full advantage his high cheekbones, deep-brown eyes and tanned good looks.

Erin poured a mug of coffee for him and carried it and a huge slice of cake to the table. He smelled soapy and fresh, without a hint of the musky aftershave he sometimes wore, probably because he hadn't touched a razor to his jaw.

"Looks great," he said, pulling out a chair and taking a seat. He glanced up at her. "Aren't you having any?"

"No, it's getting late. I should get Christie settled for the night."

"Will she be okay on the couch for another few minutes? I didn't get a chance to call Vicki today, and I'd like to hear about Amos's session."

"I'm sorry. Sure." But as Erin sat, Mac rose, poured her a cup of coffee and cut a thin slice of cake for her.

"Oh, I shouldn't," she protested. "I've already had some."

"Come on," he urged, grabbing a napkin from the holder on the counter. "Keep me company for a few minutes." He put it all down in front of her. "I haven't heard a human voice in the past twelve hours."

She sent him a skeptical look. "Martin and the boys didn't help you? And there wasn't one customer in the store from nine to five while you were counting soup cans?"

Chuckling, he dropped back into his chair. "Okay, except for Martin, the kids and a few shoppers, I haven't heard a human voice." He handed her the creamer. "How about it?"

Erin shook her head in defeat. A thought whispered through her that there might come a time when she wished she'd practiced saying no to him. But right now she was enjoying his company. He was so different from the grim, brusque man who'd greeted her when she arrived two weeks ago, and she wanted his friendship. She'd never had that kind of relationship with a man.

"All right," she said, picking up her fork. "I'll eat the cake. As for your granddad's session, it went great. His therapist is wonderful with him." Erin gave him a detailed description of all the exercises the therapist had Amos do, as well as the teasing banter that was becoming second nature between him and Vicki.

"Vicki told him he was doing so well that pretty soon the only thing he'd need his cane for was fighting off the ladies. He got so red I was afraid he was going to have another stroke."

"Lord, that's all we'd need. Actually, he does have a lady friend—for almost two years, now. Sophie Cassleback. You'd like her."

Erin put her mug down in surprise. "You're kidding. He's never mentioned her. As far as I know, they haven't even spoken on the phone since I've been here."

"That's Amos's doing. After the stroke he backed away, big-time."

"And she let him? After two years together?"

Mac gathered his dishes, setting his fork and mug on his plate. "She didn't have much choice. For a while she dropped by anyway with soups and vitamin drinks—Sophie's into herbs. But the stubborn jackass did everything but show her the door."

"How awful for both of them. She has to know why, though. He doesn't want to look weak in front of her."

"She understands that. But there's only so much of that people can take—even Sophie, and she has the patience of a saint. I saw her at the store earlier this week and we talked about the situation. I think she's close to either giving up or taking a broom to him."

Erin laughed softly, stacking her empty cup, fork and spoon on her plate, too. "Maybe we should let her."

"Maybe we should," he agreed, dark eyes twinkling.

The mini grandfather clock in the living room bonged nine times. Startled that time had flown by so quickly, Erin pushed back her chair and grabbed her dishes. She needed to get Christie into bed.

Mac stood at the same time.

And instantly their lighthearted conversation came to an end.

Only inches apart, their wary gazes locked, chemistry swirled, and Erin shivered at the knowledge she saw in Mac's eyes. She suspected the same thing was reflected in hers. They knew full well that much of their talk was only that—words and stories to distract them from what they really wanted to do. Touch. It had worked fine…until now.

Mac returned his mug and plate to the table, then he took Erin's and did the same.

Her heart beat triple time. Reluctantly she tried to back away. "Mac—"

"Shh," he whispered, threading his fingertips through the wispy tendrils at her temples, taking her right hand with his left. "It's okay."

What was okay about it? They were headed for trouble. And why wasn't she pulling her hand away as he gently coaxed her closer to him?

Their bodies melded together, fitting too well for their pairing to be a simple accident of nature. It was as though fate had made a decision, and they were powerless to stop it. Still, Erin tried.

"This isn't a good idea," she murmured as his warm hands stroked her back, then slid to her hips and bumped her even closer.

But his rugged face kept drifting nearer, his hooded gaze locked on hers. "Maybe," he whispered, "but it's not a bad one." He nipped at the corner of her mouth. "The only bad idea is putting this off any longer."

Then he was covering her mouth with his own, first tentatively seeking a response, then deepening the kiss and hungrily taking what he wanted when she gave herself over to it. His arms tightened around her and his kiss gained new depth as his tongue plumbed her mouth and mated with hers, then thrust sleekly again, claiming her, seducing her, making her quiver with a need that had been building since the day they'd met.

Erin inhaled deeply, and that quivering pooled in her belly as a new, tantalizing scent invaded her nostrils. There was that musky smell she'd missed, not from aftershave, but from him. Pheromones? she wondered in that part of her mind that still clung to clear thought. Was that it?

The second kiss became a third, the third became a fourth, and soon she was spinning mindlessly out of control.

Mac slid a hand to her bottom, pressing her to his arousal, shaping her to him as they began the dance. Coarse denim stroked thin cotton sheeting; hormones sang to the slow bumping rhythm that preceded love making.

He slid his hand up between them, burrowed under her knit top to the elastic band of her bra. Erin shivered as his hand cupped her through cotton and lace, and his tongue continued that clever, plunging preview of what was to come.

Then suddenly she was filling her hands with him, too, relishing the feel of his sturdy shoulders and strong, tapering back. She slid her hands into his back pockets. It had been so long since she'd been free to experience this part of life, this part of loving a man.

With Mac there would be equality—equal touching and pleasing. Loving him would be a banquet for the senses. With Charles—

Erin sprang away as Charles's defiant face and chilling vow shot into her mind, reminding her that she wasn't free to feel any of those things. She would *never* be free. Her mortified gaze flashed to Mac's as he blinked in confusion.

''Terri, what's—''

''I…I can't.'' She swallowed and backed away, then flushed as she pulled her top back down and smoothed her hair. It was no longer in a sedate bun at the nape of her neck.

Mac closed the short distance between them. ''You're afraid Christie or Amos will wake up.''

Actually, that hadn't even entered her mind! Would it have, in time?

''And you're right,'' he said, keeping his voice low, not waiting for her answer. ''We shouldn't have started this here. Let's get Christie into bed first.''

Erin started to object, but Mac touched the tip of his index finger to her puffy lips…stroked them softly…delved inside to touch the tip of her tongue.

''Amos sleeps like a log,'' he murmured, apparently believing that to be her next concern. ''He'll be fine alone for a half hour. If he does wake up, there's an intercom beside his bed, and one in my room at the house. We'll hear him.''

Erin eased his finger away, her mind finally clearing, though her body continued to throb. He had it all figured out, right down to the amount of time they'd need to satisfy each other. Moving away from him again, she searched her hair for her hairpins, then twisted and pinned her tangled strands into a knot again. "I'm sorry, Mac. This isn't going to happen."

It took a long second for her words to sink in. Then he said, "All right. Can you tell me why?"

"I just—a lot of reasons."

He was entitled to an explanation, but she couldn't tell him Charles would kill her if she ever let another man touch her. *I'll know if you betray me, Erin. I have many friends...and they have many friends. You belong to me. You will always belong to me.*

It was ridiculous to imagine that he had a network of people who reported to him, but what if it was true? He was a powerful man. He even had a contact on the Chicago police force, the way he'd learned that she'd taken Christie to a safe house.

She met the confusion in Mac's eyes again. How could she tell him anything about her life with Charles and keep his respect? More to the point, how could she tell him anything, period? Her attraction to him went beyond anything she'd ever felt for a man, but he was still very much a stranger to her. She'd only known him for two weeks, and it took longer than that to establish trust. Christie had to be her first priority. One innocent word to the wrong person could turn their lives into a living hell.

"Terri, if you're afraid of getting pregnant, I wouldn't have let that happen."

Another thing she hadn't considered.

Frustration lined Mac's face when she remained silent, and grave thoughts moved through his eyes. Presently, something seemed to dawn on him. "You're married, aren't you? You said Christie's father was no longer with you, but you were only speaking in physical terms. You're still legally tied to him."

"No," she replied quietly, "I'm divorced. I have been for over a year."

"Then why?" Mac persisted. "And don't tell me you don't want to sleep with me. You were as into it as I was."

Heat rose in her cheeks.

"Terri, this isn't about a gold band and forever. It's about two people who like each other spending a little time together. That's all. I'm not looking for more than that, and I suspect you aren't, either."

Faintly hurt by what he'd said, Erin glanced away. "I know it wouldn't have been about a gold band and forever." Even if she wanted it that way, which she didn't. She had to move on. But when she did, she didn't want to leave with regrets, and that could happen if they made love.

"And that's part of the problem," she continued, hoping the reason she was about to give would satisfy him, because it was a valid one. "I don't want to be a convenience. I'm too handy, living in your house, taking care of your grandfather…"

He stared, insulted. "I don't think of you that way."

"Maybe not. But I'll be leaving in a few weeks, and I…I need for my values to be intact when I go. Making love is a serious step for me. I don't sleep around. There hasn't been anyone in my life since I left my—" She couldn't bring herself to call Charles her husband. It sullied the word. "Since my divorce."

Mac stilled, digesting what she'd said. Then he blew out a ragged breath. His mind got the message, but his body wasn't in an understanding mood. What the hell had just happened here? A minute ago they were clawing at each other like animals in a cave. Now they were talking about values.

In the silence, the ticking of the grandfather clock on Amos's wall was almost deafening. He looked at her again, so beautiful, so apologetic and lost.

But values were important to him, too, and when the sick heat in his belly finally went away, maybe he'd even respect her decision. Maybe. "I'll carry Christie down to the house," he said, heading for the living room.

"I really am sorry," she murmured. "It wasn't fair of me to let it go that far."

He paused in the doorway. "Don't worry about it. I should have backed off when you hedged the first time. And you were right—it *wasn't* a good idea." Then he repeated, "I'll get Christie," because there didn't seem to be anything else to say.

Thin moonlight spangled the water as Mac crouched on the bank of the pond, listening to the distant yip and howl of the coyotes and the incessant ringing of the crickets. He'd tucked Christie into bed and left before their stilted conversation could get any more uncomfortable than it was. She'd said thank you for carrying Christie to the house; he'd said you're welcome. She'd said good-night, see you in the morning; he'd said the same.

Not even close to the way he'd envisioned their evening ending.

Feeling around in the darkness for a flat stone, he sent it skipping over the water's surface to join the others he'd tossed. One by one he watched the lights go out in his home. He missed his own bed tonight. More than that, he missed the woman who now slept in it. He'd been thinking optimistically earlier when he'd thought his need for her would fade. His nerves were shot and his stomach was a rock.

The reason she'd given him was solid. She had principles, and he liked that. But she'd also said there were a *lot* of reasons, and that made him wonder what the others were. It also made him remember how little he knew about her. Whenever they talked, they discussed food, the weather, Amos's PT sessions or something Christie had said or done that day. She never offered information about her past, other than mentioning that her mother was deceased and her father was "somewhere."

Mac swore quietly as his mind filled with suspicions he should never have put aside. Doubts that he and his hormones had been happy to gloss over as Terri slid smoothly into their lives.

He winged another skipper over the pond.

He knew nothing about the woman who was caring for his grandfather. He had no idea where she'd grown up, where she'd lived or what she'd done in the years since she'd finished school. He didn't know if she'd attended college, why she'd left her husband, or if Fletcher was her married or maiden name. He didn't even know how old she was, though if he had to guess, he'd put her in her very early thirties.

A ridiculing voice rose in his mind, questioning his motives. *Any chance you're just pissed off because she said no?*

"Good chance," he muttered. Still, his uncertainties about her had to be considered.

Mac rose from the bank, dusted the dried mud from his fingers and walked back to his granddad's place, determined to find that list of references she'd given Amos. These days, no one could keep their lives secret for long. He *would* get answers to his questions, if not from her, from someone else. Because now that he thought about it, when she sprang back from him tonight, she'd looked almost...scared.

Chapter 6

Mac's grim expression kept materializing on Erin's windshield, superimposing itself over pine forests and blue skies as she drove Amos home from his Tuesday-afternoon PT session. He wasn't much company today, snoozing beside her, his head lolled at an uncomfortable-looking angle against the side window. In the back seat, Christie was also asleep, Raggedy Ann wedged into the car seat in front of her. No company there, either.

That gave her too much time to worry about Mac's probing behavior these past few days. Ever since she'd bolted away from him on Friday night, he'd been asking very thinly veiled questions about her past again. And with each new lie and half-truth she'd offered, she could see more doubt in his eyes.

She gave a nervous start as an unmarked police car suddenly swerved out of the secondary road she'd just passed and turned onto the highway, a portable strobe light flashing. With a short burst of his siren, the lone officer behind the wheel motioned her over to the side of the road.

What had she done? She couldn't have been speeding! These days she practically rode the brake, knowing it was risky to call attention to herself!

Erin glanced quickly to the right. Amos was still sleeping with his face turned to the window, and she prayed fervently that he would stay that way. Christie, too.

Pulling the van to the side of the road, she fumbled in her shoulder bag for her wallet, then with shaky fingers, managed to tug her driver's license out of it. Cautiously she took her registration and insurance cards from the glove box, then put down her window.

A nice-looking officer with sandy hair and an amiable smile walked up to her, peered in the back seat at Christie for a moment, then glanced briefly at Amos and brought his blue eyes back to her.

"Afternoon, ma'am," he said cordially.

"Good afternoon, Officer—" she read his nametag "—Kendall."

"May I see your driver's license and registration, please, ma'am?"

Nodding, she handed them over, swallowing the bile rising in her throat. The fewer words spoken, the better; the less noise, the better. She wouldn't even ask him what she'd done. She just wanted him to fine her and leave before Amos woke up!

"Be right back," he said in that same official tone.

Erin watched in the side mirror as he returned to his vehicle, presumably to check the van's ownership and search her records for outstanding warrants. No alarm bells would sound. She'd been a law-abiding citizen in Maine where she'd obtained her new driver's license, and she'd still been a law-abiding citizen in Bangor when she'd traded the white Ford Windstar in on her Dodge Caravan. Millie's brother had issued her a new plate and destroyed the old one.

She just hadn't been Terri Fletcher in either of those places.

A nauseating fear had pooled in her stomach by the time Kendall ambled back and handed her credentials through the open window.

"Ms. Fallon, the reason I pulled you over—"

Quickly, Erin raised an index finger to her lips to stop his words, and at the same time, smiled weakly and nodded toward Christie in the back seat. Another lie joined the year-long string. "My daughter gets carsick," she murmured. "I'd rather she didn't wake up until we're parked for the day."

The officer seemed to understand and lowered his voice. "There's a brake light out on your van, Ms. Fallon."

Erin kept her tone low, too. "I wasn't aware of that."

"No problem. It's hard to know that unless someone sees and alerts you. Planning to be in High Hawk long?"

Of course. With Maine plates, he would assume she was visiting or passing through. "A few weeks."

"Then you'll need to get that light fixed soon," Kendall said. "If you're stopped again, we'll have to fine you."

Amos snuffled and smacked his lips as though his mouth were dry. A jolt of adrenaline hit, and Erin's nerve endings responded. *He couldn't wake up now.*

Not yet. "I'll take care of it first thing tomorrow, Officer," she returned.

Kendall smiled. "Good. Enjoy your stay, ma'am."

"Thank you."

Everything in her crumbled in relief when Kendall finally walked away.

Slowly turning her head, Erin sent Amos a cautious look. He was still snoring softly, but now his chin rested on his chest.

Blowing out a quiet blast of air, she dropped the van into gear again and drove, her stomach still quaking. She had to calm down. In two hours Mac would close the store and come home for supper, and he'd undoubtedly see any kind of anxiety as an excuse to ask more questions.

"Where did you say you grew up?" he'd asked yesterday.

"I didn't. It was a small town in Illinois."

Then later, after he'd read about plans for the fall homecoming celebration at Arizona State: "I'll probably make it this year. Do you ever go back for yours?"

She'd never said she'd attended college, so it had been a good guess and a thoughtfully formed guess at that. No matter how she answered, it would open up a new flood of questions. She'd ended up admitting she had a masters degree in early childhood education, then lying again when he asked why she no longer taught. "Just decided to take a break and travel a while."

She couldn't tell him that Charles had manipulated her into quitting, insisting that they didn't need the money and that she was depriving someone else of employment. Relieving her of her profession had been just one more step in isolating her from her friends and making her dependent upon him. And she'd let him do it. Now her new occupation was lying for a living.

Sighing, Erin flipped on her left-turn signal and bumped off the highway onto one of the secondary roads that would lead her back to Amos's secluded little ranch.

Thank heaven she'd kept her own savings account, or she never would've been able to run as far as she had. Not on the initial settlement installment she'd been awarded. Charles and his lawyers had made sure the money wouldn't be surrendered in a lump sum, and she'd run before subsequent checks were sent.

She still had no idea why she'd kept the account a secret from him. Intuition? Some vague signal that all wasn't right with him? A signal she couldn't admit on a conscious level?

Strange, the places one found guidance. Years ago she'd seen a tag line on a tea bag that went something like, *Always tell the truth. It takes a great memory to be a good liar.*

She yearned for the day when she could take that advice.

The answering machine in Amos's living room was playing when they walked through the kitchen door fifteen minutes later. His expression turned sheepish as a woman's strident voice carried to them, soaring to new heights of aggravation.

"…so you'd better call me back damn soon, old man, or I'm coming over there. It's been two months! I'm tired of your pride and stubbornness, and I'm tired of getting information secondhand!"

Amos winced as the woman slammed the receiver onto a cradle somewhere, then he caned his way to his recliner and flumped down into it. "Well," he grumbled, "I s'pose I'd better call her."

"Lady friend?" Erin asked, briefly setting aside her anxiety at nearly being found out today. She was fairly certain she knew who the caller was, but she wondered what Amos would say. Across the room, Christie was already jabbering to the pile of stuffed animals she'd left near the TV set.

"Sophie Casselback," Amos answered. "The bossiest woman on God's green earth."

"But you like her."

Scowling, he pulled the phone from the end table onto his lap. "No, I put up with her." A long moment passed while he paused with his hand on the receiver, then he jerked a look up at her. "You gonna monitor this conversation?"

Erin grinned, pulling herself up short. "No, I'm going to start dinner." She held out a hand to Christie. "Come on, sweetie. Let's wash up. Mommy needs some help today."

"I'n a good helper!"

"Yes, you are."

A few minutes later, as Erin scrubbed and oiled big russet potatoes to go with their baked haddock, and Christie tore lettuce for salads, she heard shreds of an argument, then the softer tones of a man who cared about a woman. She couldn't hear much, and honestly wasn't eavesdropping. But it was fairly clear from the few words she heard that Sophie would be paying a call on Amos in the next few days.

Smiling a little, Erin popped the potatoes in the oven. She'd have to tell Mac that letting Sophie take a broom to Amos might not be necessary after all. Maybe a light conversation over dinner would clear some of the edginess from their mutual air, and get them back on friendlier footing.

It didn't. In fact, Mac seemed even more distant and preoccupied than usual when he came home. Even Amos noticed.

"You get up on the wrong side o' the bed this morning?" he asked as Mac left the table and carried his dishes to the sink.

"The bed's pushed against the wall," Mac replied succinctly. "I can only get out of one side."

"Then we'd best move the bed," Amos declared. Earlier he'd insisted that if he ate fish one more time he'd sprout fins, but from the way he shoveled it into his mouth, Erin suspected he'd only growled because it was expected of him.

She watched Mac rinse his plate and silverware, then reach inside the cupboard to his left where mugs were stored. His broad shoulders strained the fabric of his burgundy shirt as he worked. "Sorry for my mood," he muttered. "I got a disturbing phone call this afternoon at the store."

Amos jerked his attention up from his dinner. "If Vicki said I didn't try hard enough today, she's lyin'."

For the first time since he'd walked in, a slight smile tipped the corners of Mac's mouth. "It wasn't about you, Granddad. When I called this afternoon, Vicki said your session went exceptionally well." He took the short pitcher of cream from the refrigerator, removed the lid. "I told you that Shane called the other day."

"To catch up, you said."

"To catch up, and to ask if I'd like to join him in a new business venture."

Amos stilled, chewed more slowly, then looked up. There was a hesitance, an uncertainty in his eyes and voice. "You goin' back to New Hampshire?"

"No, he's coming here. Arizona's still growing by leaps and bounds, and Shane believes the area's ripe for another civil engineering firm. Supposedly, the state's going to need to replace a few highways, bridges and viaducts that require professional engineers with experience. There are also a few dozen construction and manufacturing jobs going up for bid."

Erin blinked. "You build bridges?"

"Bridges, shopping centers, water treatment plants…" The look he sent her couldn't have been any more candid or straightforward. "*My* life's an open book."

She stared back for a time, letting him know she'd gotten the message. Then she averted her gaze, pulled her chair closer to Christie's booster seat and took her fork away. "Come on, honey," she murmured, stabbing a piece of haddock, "you need to eat a little more before we have dessert."

"No! I don't wike it!"

"You liked it two minutes ago," Erin reminded her, extending the fork. Christie slapped it away, and it bounced across the table.

"Christie Lynn!"

"I want ice cweam!"

Sighing, mentally counting to ten, Erin retrieved the fork. She didn't need a temper tantrum today. Not after being grilled for days by Mac and nearly found out by Amos this afternoon. "All right, you don't have to eat the fish. Try some of the nice salad you made."

"No!"

Amos chuckled. "Maybe her bed needs t' be pulled away from the wall, too."

As Christie renewed her objections to healthy food, he spoke to Mac again. "Hope you told Shane you'd do it. You been away from the business too long. Time you got your feet wet again."

"It's not an easy decision," Mac replied, reaching for the pot. "Coffee?"

"It ain't coffee, it's decaf, and don't change the subject. Why is it a hard decision t' make?"

"Because I'm not ready yet, and he's been approached by a colleague who got wind of his plan and wants in. Now, do you want a cup or don't you?"

"Yeah, I want a cup, and why ain't you ready? It's because of me, ain't it? You think you can't make plans till I get back to work."

Becoming more frustrated by the moment, Erin turned away from Christie's bulging cheeks and thundercloud expression. She was now accepting food but refusing to swallow.

Erin was surprised but touched when Mac set a mug down in front of her. Their relationship was a mess, but he'd still poured her coffee and added just the right amount of cream.

She murmured a thank-you just as Christie opened her mouth wide and let the salad simply fall out of it.

"All right," Erin said standing abruptly, "somebody's going to bed."

"No!" Christie screeched, and started to cry.

"Yes."

Mac stared, obviously bewildered. "Is she sick?"

"No, she's not three yet." Lifting Christie out of the booster chair, Erin strode toward the bathroom to wash her face and hands and have a much-needed discussion with her daughter about acceptable behavior. ''You've heard of the terrible twos?'' she called over Christie's bellowing. ''This is it.''

When she returned to the kitchen a few minutes later, Christie was snuffling but had finally calmed down, so Erin relaxed her ruling on early bedtime. After sitting her in her booster chair, she gave her a container of fruited yogurt for dessert, then started the dishes.

Mac and Amos had cleared the table and gone into the living room. Fitting the plug into the drain, Erin turned on the taps and squirted lemon dishwashing liquid into the water.

A minute later Mac ambled back into the kitchen. She felt his warmth along her back as he slid his coffee cup into the sink. His voice was another matter. It wasn't brusque, but it wasn't friendly, either.

''Go ahead and take Christie home.''

''I will. As soon as I finish straightening the kitchen.''

''I'll do the dishes tonight.''

''This is my job,'' she returned, keeping her gaze on the bubbles and the glasses she was washing. ''I'll do them.''

Christie let out another wail.

Briefly closing her eyes, then wiping her wet hands on her jeans, Erin strode to the table. Somehow Christie'd gotten yogurt in her hair. Grabbing a napkin, she daubed it away. ''Honey,'' she said through a sigh, ''I thought you were going to be a happy girl now.''

''I don't wike da fwoot! I wike peaches!''

''Christie, those are peaches.''

Mac came to the table, his tone finally softening.

"Take her home and get her ready for bed. Maybe playing with her toys in the bathtub will help."

"When I'm finished."

"Terri—"

"Mac," she returned, glaring now.

He sighed in annoyance. "All right, do the dishes. But let me take Christie for a walk. I need to use my computer for a few minutes—check my e-mail and get Shane's phone number from my files." His gaze shifted to Christie's pouting expression. "I'm pretty sure she's had it with the yogurt."

Suddenly, having someone else deal with Christie seemed like a very good idea. For the past few days she'd been an absolute angel. But today, when Erin was still wired from her encounter with Officer Kendall, Christie just had to sprout horns.

"Thank you," she said, grateful for the help. "I'd love it if you took her for a walk. Just let me wash her hands and face again."

She was a model child by the time they passed the pond, talking nonstop about swimming and playing there yesterday. "My Bobbies got too wet!"

"I know. I saw them." Mac grinned down at her. "Guess what, Christie?"

"What?"

"In a few days I think there's going to be a surprise down at the barn."

"Candy?"

"No, kitties. One of our mommy cats is going to have some babies."

She shrieked excitedly, and he promised to show her when they arrived. Then they were entering the house, and Christie was running into the great room off the foyer to see if her Barbie dolls had dried. Mac watched her drop to her knees on one of the woven Navajo rugs covering his hardwood floor, then open a small suitcase bulging with dolls and clothes. "Christie, I'll be in the computer room. Okay?"

"Okay."

He checked and answered his e-mail, except for a message from a friend who wanted him to participate in a charity softball game. That, like Shane's offer, required some thought. Then he carefully examined his junk mail before he deleted them.

Mac frowned. Funny. For someone who'd wanted to e-mail her friends, Terri wasn't receiving any replies. Or maybe she'd already deleted their messages. He stared a few moments longer, thinking about how secretive she was...half hearing Christie singing nursery rhymes across the hall. One click of his mouse could take him to his computer's trash bin to check the messages that had been deleted. Unless she'd deleted them from the trash bin, too.

His index finger stroked the mouse, struggling with temptation. He'd looked high and low for that slip of paper listing her references but hadn't been able to find it. He'd finally asked Amos, but the old man denied knowing what had happened to it.

Muttering a curse, Mac shut down the computer, took his address book with Shane's new phone number in it from the desk drawer and jammed it into his shirt pocket. Any information he learned about her would have to come from another source. Accessing her e-mail was too invasive.

"Christie?" he called rolling his chair back from the desk and standing. "Ready to go?"

She yelled back something about taking her Barbies and clothes with her. He almost told her to leave them here because she'd be coming back down in a few minutes, but he didn't want any more tears.

"Okay," he answered, coming into the great room.

Christie's small brow furrowed as she tried to wrestle everything she'd taken from the suitcase back into it. "I fink my Bobbies have too much clothes," she said, grunting to close it.

Mac crouched beside her. "Want some help?"

She shook her head no and grunted louder.

The scent of vanilla tinged the air, coming from the apothecary-jar candle sitting on an end table. In fact, now that he glanced around, he saw several touches that Terri had added. Baskets of dried wildflowers sat here and there, various photographs of Christie topped the table near his fieldstone fireplace, and throw pillows in earthy shades brightened his brown overstuffed sofa. With only a few trappings, she'd made his house a home.

"Unco Mac, you do it."

He grinned at the name they'd finally agreed on. "Mr. Corbett" was too formal for him; just plain "Mac" wasn't formal enough for Terri. Amos was now "Papa Amos."

"Give it here," he said, then stuffed everything inside the hard case and snapped the locks into place.

He was lifting it when his eyes narrowed on the gold initials on the bag. Three letters, all in big, loopy script.

Not one of those letters worked with a name like Terri Fletcher.

By the time he and Christie reached Amos's house, Mac's mood was as dark as Christie's had been earlier.

He herded Christie into the living room, asked Amos to keep her occupied for a few minutes, then took the broom out of Terri's hand, propped it in the corner beside the door and led her out on the porch.

Releasing his grip on her wrist, he snapped, "What's your real name?"

Erin stared, her heartbeat racing. What was going on? What had he found at the house that told him she'd been lying? She hadn't yet e-mailed Millie or Lynn, so he couldn't have discovered anything from the computer. "You know my name," she said, working to keep her voice calm.

He stared down at her with cold, cold eyes. "Do I? Terri Fletcher?"

She nodded, feeling backed into a corner.

"Then why are the initials on your luggage C. L. R.?"

Relief flooded her. So that's what he'd found. "Obviously because the person who once owned it *did* have those initials," she answered truthfully. "I bought it at a yard sale during our travels."

He didn't believe her. She could see it on his face. "I seriously doubt that you found something that nice at a yard sale. It's practically brand-new."

Suddenly Erin exploded in a temper that matched his. She didn't have a right to because she *had* been lying to him. But it had been such a horrid day, and between the brake light fiasco, Mac's foul mood and Christie's tantrum, she was so unhinged, she gave him both barrels.

"Well, guess what? I did find something that nice at a yard sale. Would you like to know how much I paid for it? Three dollars. Well worth the price, don't you think?" She took in a breath, unable to stop herself from lashing out. "Why can't you believe a solitary thing I say? You've been grilling me since I got here, and no matter how I answer, I see doubt in your eyes. Well, it's getting old! Is there something I'm doing wrong? Because if you have any objections about the way I care for your grandfather, wash your clothes or mash your potatoes, now's the time to say so!''

Shaking inside and out, she glared up at him, watching his expression go from angry, to stunned.

Neither of them spoke for a long, solemn moment. Then finally Mac said, ''I'm sorry,'' and went back inside the house.

Erin stayed where she was, her hands practically wringing pine sap out of the porch rail while she struggled for calm. But as those physical problems came under control, she suddenly felt sick to her stomach remembering his apologetic look.

Dear God, what a mess she'd made of everything. She was now the worst liar in the world because there was a chance she'd convinced him that she was honorable—and she was miles from that.

Swallowing, she went back inside, took her broom from the corner, then briefly glanced in the direction of the coffeemaker. Mac was refilling his cup, his expression stony. Then, wordlessly, he grabbed a magazine from the living room, carried his coffee past her and returned to the porch.

She felt as though she might throw up.

Amos and Christie came silently into the kitchen, Christie's eyes wide and uncertain, Amos wearing a sympathetic expression. They would've had to be deaf to miss her outburst.

Setting the broom aside, Erin lifted Christie into her arms and held her close. ''I'm sorry, sweetheart,'' she murmured as her daughter's arms and legs wrapped around her. "Mommy was just upset for a minute. But I'm not upset with you." Erin smoothed Christie's hair and kissed it, then snuggled her on her shoulder. She met Amos's eyes. "I'm sorry."

"Don't be," he said, squeezing her arm on his way to the counter.

Erin spoke quickly when she realized he was about to fill his coffee mug, too. "Amos, wait. Let me get that for you."

"Nah, you cuddle yer little one," he replied. "It'll do me good t' get my own." He hooked his cane over his right wrist then used his left hand to pour. "About Mac..." he began, then paused to return the carafe to the unit, "sometimes he gets my dander up, too."

He grabbed his cup, a little decaf slopping over the rim as he cane tapped his way toward her. "I suspect he gets himself all wrapped up in unimportant stuff 'cause he don't have enough goin' on in his own life." He winked at Erin and lowered his voice as he went to the door. "He just needs a little distractin'."

When the screen door banged shut behind him, Erin unhooked Christie's legs from around her waist, then draped them over her thighs as she sank to a chair.

Mac wasn't the only one who needed more in his life. She needed a distraction as badly as he did. And how she wished they could distract each other. A lot of her tension was directly related to the knots in her stomach that simply wouldn't go away—and the hurt in her heart that he didn't trust her, whether she deserved his trust or not. She cared what he thought of her, cared too much.

Erin looked down at her droopy-eyed daughter; she was all worn-out from her happy-sad day. It was easy for Erin to relate.

"Hey, sleepy girl," she murmured. "Let's take some dessert out to Uncle Mac and Papa Amos, then go find Raggedy Ann and get ready for bed. Does that sound like a good idea?"

Christie nodded and yawned.

A few minutes later Christie tagged along behind her as Erin placed a thin slice of apple pie, a napkin and a fork on the parson's table near Amos's chair. A dozen feet away, Mac lounged in a second chair, reading. His boots were propped up on the porch rail. There was no table beside him so Erin waited until he'd met her eyes, pulled his feet down and put his magazine aside. Then she handed him a plate. The fork she gave him had a white paper napkin pinched between the tines. A flag of truce.

He accepted both.

"I'm sorry," she said quietly. "I didn't have to get so passionate about the whole thing."

Mac kept his voice low and his sober gaze on hers. "It's okay. A little passion never hurt anybody."

That familiar airy feeling twirled through her stomach, and her heart skipped a beat. Maybe not. But any passion he had to give would have to be shared with someone else.

Still, his words turned the night into dreams, and they were dreams that made her pulse race and her body ache.

For him.

Chapter 7

Erin glanced up from scanning the want ads in yesterday's paper as the screen door creaked long and loud on its hinges, and Amos came outside. At the far end of the porch, Christie was building a castle with Legos, but her dollies and stuffed animals were stretched out beside Erin on the old green-and-yellow metal glider—doing their penance for being cranky all morning.

As the screen door slammed, Amos pointed his cane at the want ads and settled himself into the padded Adirondack chair beside Erin. "You goin' somewheres?"

She blinked, then realized he thought she was scouting for a new job. "Nope. Not until you say so." She folded the paper and set it aside. "Did you have a good nap?"

"Fair t' middlin'," he answered, then reached

across the parson's table between them to hand her an envelope.

"What's this?"

"Open it."

With a brief, curious look at him, she opened the envelope and pulled out a thick wad of bills. Blinking, she met his hazel eyes again. "Money?"

"It's yer pay. I hope yer okay with cash. Can't find my checkbook."

Cash was a godsend! She wouldn't have to sign Terri's name to a check. She'd been worrying about using her deceased friend's identity and social security number since she'd left Maine. Then a troubling thought occurred to her. "Amos, I…I thought we'd agreed that I'd be paid at the end of the month."

"Oh? I don't recall sayin' that. Just figured y'd been with us three weeks, and it was high time you got some pay for yer time. Count it, now. Make sure that's the amount we agreed on."

She had no intention of counting it. Suddenly nervous, Erin slipped the bills back into the envelope, her mind racing. Was it just a coincidence that yesterday a police officer had called her Ms. Fallon, and today Amos was handing her cash instead of a check? Had he overheard…and sensed her fear? Was he now trying to help her keep her identity a secret? If so, why? And if he thought he knew something, why wasn't he asking her about it?

Standing, she moistened her lips and swallowed, all the moisture gone from her throat. "Thank you, Amos. I'll tuck this in my purse, then I'll look for your checkbook. Did you have it with you when we went to Flagstaff yesterday?"

"Nah, it ain't been around for a while. It'll turn up.

Mac prob'ly put it someplace. I'll ask him when he comes home.''

"All right,'' she said. "But if you change your mind, I'll start looking.'' Thoughts of their ride home yesterday reminded her that her van still needed some attention. "Amos, I need to have a light replaced in my van. Could you suggest a garage that would do it?''

"Sure. You kin take it t' Everett Hodge's place on Main Street, just up from my store. But it ain't a hard job. Mac can bring a bulb home.''

"I don't want to put him out.''

"Y' wouldn't be. Won't take him but a minute to fix it. Besides, Everett's only open till five. You'd have to wait till Saturday to get it done.'' He sent her a sarcastic look. "Unless you figured on leavin' me without a keeper for an hour.''

She smiled. "I'm sure you'd be fine by yourself, but Mac would string us both up if I did that.'' She glanced at her watch; it wasn't quite 2 p.m. "Would you mind riding into town with me now? Maybe Mr. Hodge would have time to do it.''

Shrugging, Amos grabbed his cane and hoisted himself up with a hand on the arm of his chair. "Guess I could do that. It'd give me a chance t'see what the front of my store's lookin' like these days.''

The garage at the corner of Main and Taylor had a decidedly old-fashioned look. In fact, the entire town did, as she'd discovered when she'd first arrived. With the exception of the small brick bank, High Hawk's business section—if you could call it that—consisted mainly of painted clapboard, false front buildings with long plate-glass windows. There were even a few ancient gas pumps with round heads and red bodies stationed at the front of Hodge's weathered gray garage for flavor.

A balding, heavyset man with a fringe of gray hair chuckled when he saw Amos in the van and walked across the dirt lot to talk, wiping his hands on a coarse orange rag. He stuffed the rag in the back pocket of his stained coveralls as one of his men went to change the bulb.

His voice boomed cheerfully. "This your new girlfriend, Amos?"

Amos grinned. "Yep, we're gettin' hitched, soon as I hit the lottery." He glanced at Erin. "Terri, this here's Everett Hodge, the crookedest pinochle player in the state. Hodge, this is Terri Fletcher, my new jailer."

"Pleased to meet you." The mechanic's blue eyes twinkled. "This old liar needs a jailer." He looked at Amos, affection in his gaze. "How you doin', Amos?"

"Still got my hair. How's yer day goin'?"

"Good, good." He chuckled again. "They're all good when we wake up above ground."

Fifteen minutes later as they drove out of the lot, Amos settled back against his seat with a husky laugh. "Felt good t'chew the fat with old Everett, though y'can't believe a blamed word he says. Been a storyteller since I met him."

Erin smiled, pleased to see him this way. "Well, if that was fun, how would you like to go into your store instead of just looking at the outside?" Christie was snoozing in her car seat, but she could wake her. "You might run into a few of your customers. They'd probably love to—"

"No." His reply was sharp and succinct, and color flared in his cheeks.

Nevertheless, when she approached the yellow clapboard general store with its high-flying sign, Erin eased the van off the road and stopped on the edge of the cinder lot, hoping Amos would change his mind.

She wanted to see Mac.

There, she'd admitted it. Things were strained between them, but every molecule in her body wanted to look at him, stand close to him…eat chocolate cake with him.

Then she saw the five concrete steps with the black pipe handrail leading to the front door, and realized Amos would have a difficult time climbing them. He'd had no trouble sitting in her van with Everett Hodge poked half inside the window, slinging good-natured insults and renewing their friendship. But his pride wouldn't let him get out of the van and let people see his infirmity.

Still hoping he'd reconsider, she read aloud the legend on the dark-green sign with gold letters, thinking there was probably a back door for deliveries that would be more easily accessible. "Clarence M. Perkins & Sons, Established 1927. Is that right?"

"Yep," he answered, glancing around with a why-ain't-we-movin' look on his face. "My granddaddy opened it just before the Great Depression. Been in the family ever since. I expect I'll be the last Perkins to own it. My brother's kids ain't interested in nothin' but oil rigs and makin' money."

"You have family in…Texas?" Erin guessed.

He grunted an affirmative. "My brother Jeremiah. Changed his name to Jerome and married a gal from Houston right after high school. She had the damnedest hair I ever seen. Brown with a big hunk of blond down one side—and it was natural, mind you." His tone softened and grew faintly nostalgic. "But he made a good life for himself and her...had a coupla boys and built a nice house. As for him changin' his name..." He met Erin's eyes. "Well, I guess that was all right. He's still the same person. Just a little shorter on the syllables."

A shiver chased down her spine. Was he trying to tell her that he knew her name wasn't Terri—and that it was all right with him? Or was the tale of his Texas brother just another story, like the ones he'd been swapping with Everett Hodge?

When she didn't speak for a moment, Amos did, his trademark growl back in place. "You gonna lollygag all day, missy, or step on that gas pedal? I'm missin' *Gunsmoke.*"

Relieved to let it go at that, Erin backed out of the cindered lot. But not before she saw Mac and another man wander onto the loading dock of a large, tan, corrugated-steel building behind and to the left of the store. The sign over the wide doorway read: Feed & Seed. Mac spotted them at the same moment, and paused in his conversation to stare soberly.

With a slight wave, Erin eased onto the road again and headed for home, too many tingles and twitches in her belly to blame solely on what Amos did or did not know. She wanted Mac Corbett. She wanted him at night, she wanted him in the morning, and she wanted him now. What on earth did people do with hormones that refused to listen to reason?

You know, a small voice murmured deep in her mind.

Yes, she did. *They gave into it.*

The mere thought of loving him in the darkness made Erin miss her next turn.

Supper was a quiet affair that night. Mac asked Amos why he hadn't stopped at the store after their visit to the garage, and Amos said he was missing his TV programs. They all spoke cordially, with Mac accepting everything she said without question—and making her feel guilty all over again.

Immediately after the meal he helped her clear the table and stack the dishes, then excused himself to feed and water the stock. It was all very civilized, and yet, as Erin walked Christie down the slight grade to Mac's log home later, she felt the ever-widening gulf between them.

Isn't that what you wanted? her conscience prodded.

Yes, but…

There are no buts. When he kisses you, you ask him to stop. When he keeps his distance, you don't like that, either. Make up your mind.

"Easier said than done," she murmured.

"What, Mommy?"

"Nothing, sweet pea," she returned with a weary smile. "Just thinking out loud."

She was so edgy and at loose ends that night after Christie fell asleep, she had to talk to someone. The pull to connect with friends was strong, but contacting anyone was dangerous. She still wasn't certain of how Charles's P.I. had found her in Maine, though she thought it might have been through her first van purchase.

Drawing a deep breath, telling herself that there was no reason to believe anyone was monitoring Millie's home phone line, she calculated the time in the east, pulled a department store phone card from her wallet and started tapping in numbers.

Erin was stunned to hear tears in Millie's voice when she answered.

"Millie what's wrong?" she asked in alarm. At sixty-six, Millie was the most upbeat woman she'd ever known. Tears and Millie Kraft did not go together unless they were tears of happiness, and these were not.

The older woman's voice changed to a cautious hush. "Are you all right?"

"Yes," Erin replied, aware that Millie hadn't used her name. "What's happening there?"

"Oh, honey," she said, tears giving way again. "It's the most terrible thing. Trisha's dead!"

"Oh, Millie, no!"

"Yes. Lobstermen found her body floating in the bay early yesterday morning when they were casting off. Apparently, she'd been swimming. She was wearing a bathing suit."

"Dear God," Erin breathed. "Then...it was a drowning accident?"

"It looks that way...but honey, there was this man, this stranger she'd been seeing..."

The hairs on the back of Erin's neck stood on end. "What does Trisha's seeing a man have to do with her death?"

"Probably nothing, but the water's still cold this time of year, and I keep thinking that someone would have had to do some fancy talking to interest her in a moonlight swim. Besides...I never liked that man's looks. For one thing, he was too old for her, and for another..." Millie seemed to weigh the wisdom of continuing, then did. "For another, he'd asked her questions about another waitress who used to work for me. A sweet young woman who left a few weeks ago. I wanted to contact her immediately, but I didn't know how to reach her.''

Erin's nerves rioted. "Th-the man," she stammered. "Early forties, dark, reddish-brown hair, green eyes? Fine mustache and Vandyke beard?''

Millie continued in a low tone. "No, he had medium-brown hair, but it might've been dyed because the color looked uneven in the sun. I only saw him from a distance, so I don't know about his eyes. But he mostly wore sunglasses. And I think he was younger than forty. But, as I said, he asked questions about another waitress. Trisha said she'd even accused him of being more interested in the other girl, but he assured her that he was only curious because the other waitress had been so friendly and he'd thought her little girl was the cutest he'd ever seen.''

Chills covered every inch of Erin's skin. Yes, she'd always been friendly to her customers. And yes, she'd taken Christie to work with her on several occasions instead of leaving her at the nursery school, so the man's statement was probably true. But she had good reason to fear this much interest. What other information had Trisha shared with the stranger? Millie and Lynn were the only two people she'd taken into her confidence, and only because Lynn had helped her escape, and Millie had carefully, lovingly drawn her out. Even then it had taken five months for Erin to open up to her.

And now…Trisha was dead. Tears filled Erin's eyes. *Please,* she begged in her mind. *Please don't let it be because of me. Please don't let this man be connected to Charles.*

She drew a deep breath, pulled herself together. "Millie, do you know if she told him anything that...that might put the woman's daughter at risk?"

"I don't know. She did learn something accidentally when she took a phone message for me, but I can't say if she shared the information. And, honey, she wouldn't have known it could be dangerous to mention."

"What information?"

"Information about a new vehicle."

Blood pounded in Erin's temples and throat. Someone *might* know that she'd traded in her white van for an older gray one? Was that enough to trace her?

"Honey?"

"I...I'm here."

"Remember, early reports point to accidental drowning. Keep that in mind."

"Yes. Yes, I will." She had to or she would lose her mind. Suddenly it was all too much. She'd phoned Millie to hear a friendly voice, to soothe her unhappiness. And now there was grief over Trisha's death, guilt that it could be connected to her, and a new fear that they could be found and she would lose Christie to a monster.

You think you've won, Erin? he'd said smoothly after her court appearance. *Don't delude yourself. I will have what's mine, no matter how long it takes, or how many people get hurt in the process. You included.*

Her heart raced. "Millie, I have to go."

"Are you well?"

"Yes."

"Be careful, honey."

"I will."

Erin clattered the receiver onto the cradle and ran

to the bedroom, pulled her suitcase from the closet and yanked open a drawer. She'd emptied them all by the time she realized she couldn't leave.

Sinking to the bed, she dropped her head onto her lap and wept. She had obligations here! She couldn't just leave Amos without a caregiver, not after telling him she would stay as long as he needed her! And Mac... Her heart ached so much more than it should at the thought of leaving him. But if Trisha's death wasn't an accident, and Charles was somehow responsible, she could be putting Amos and Mac at risk for simply knowing her.

Stop it! You're letting fear take over. All you really know is, a stranger Millie didn't like was asking questions about you, and he might have received information about your new van from Trisha.

Which reinforced again how dangerous it was to share anything of a personal nature—with *anyone*. All it took was one slip of the tongue to someone who repeated it to someone else, and she and Christie could be found.

Erin bolted from the bed, rushing to every room in the house to check the locks on the doors and windows. Then, chilled to the bone, she crawled into Christie's narrow bed, tugged the granny afghan up from the bottom and snuggled her daughter into the curve of her body.

The sweet smells of baby shampoo and talc nearly made her cry again. Erin fought for control. It would be a long time until sleep came, but that was all right. She had to gather her thoughts. She had to make plans.

Erin never heard the short, staccato beeping of the alarm clock from across the hall until Christie crawled on top of her, brought her sweet face close, and tried to pry open her eyes.

"Oh, honey, don't do that," she groaned, then smiled sleepily and wrapped her daughter in her arms. "Good morning special girl," Erin whispered.

"G'mornin', special Mommy," Christie whispered back. "The cwock is beeping."

"Then we'd better shut it off," Erin returned, kissing Christie's upturned nose.

But she was scarcely out of bed when last night's conversation with Millie came back with a vengeance, and her nerves caught fire again. She managed to hide her fear from Christie and Amos as she fixed, then joined them for breakfast. She wasn't as successful with Mac.

Chills erupted on her arms when he came into the narrow pantry off the kitchen where she was putting away the oatmeal and syrup.

His voice was low and deep. "What's wrong with you this morning?"

"Nothing."

"Bull. You've been dropping things and racing around like a roadrunner on speed. You haven't drawn a calm breath since you walked in this morning. Something happened."

"You're imagining things." She tried to brush past him, but he caught her around the waist and kept her inside the claustrophobic confines, away from Amos's eyes and ears.

Erin met his grave expression, feeling the warmth of his hands through her cotton blouse. Her gaze flicked over his chiseled features and sensual mouth...and her pulse increased. She didn't need the added confusion of chemistry today. "Let me go."

''Not until you tell me why you're acting this way. Are you still angry because I went off on you the other day?''

Unable to look at him and deliver yet another lie, she looked past him to the canned goods stocked on the opposite shelf. ''No, I...I didn't sleep well last night and I have a headache. Now, please...I just want to finish straightening up the kitchen and get some meds from my purse before it gets any worse.''

''Where's your purse?''

''At the—at your house.''

''I'll get you some ibuprofen from Amos's medicine cabinet.''

''No!'' Seeing how startled he was by her reaction, she calmed herself. She couldn't be swallowing un-needed painkillers. ''Thank you, but I have something that works better. I'll just run down and get it before you leave to open the store.''

''You have a headache. I'll get it.''

She couldn't let him. Her open suitcase was still in his room. She hadn't had time to unpack and put it away this morning, just left it on the floor on the far side of his bed. It was out of the way, but if he saw it, he would know she'd considered running again. ''Mac, no, I'll—''

The kitchen phone shrilled over her objections. With one last curiously assessing look at her, Mac went to answer it.

''Corbett,'' he said. When the caller identified her-self and Mac heard the tension in Betty Moran's voice, he grew instantly concerned. ''Yeah, it's me, Betty. What's wrong?''

''I'm so glad you answered. I didn't want to bother Amos with this. Chip's had some trouble,'' she blurted. "But first I should tell you that he's going to be all right. His leg's broken and he has a few bruised ribs."

"Oh, damn. What happened?"

"He was riding last night and his horse got spooked by something—Chip's not sure what. It was getting dark. Anyway, Dakota threw him, and I'm afraid he won't be coming to work for a while. We know you're busy, and you're short-handed with your granddad being laid up and all, but— Mac, Chip's just sick about this."

"Tell him we'll be fine. What he needs to do right now is concentrate on getting better. Is he at home or in the hospital?"

"He's at home. It was a clean break, thank heaven."

"Does he need anything?"

Betty hesitated for a moment. "We have everything under control, I think, except…well, it would help him to know that he still has a job when he's healed. College won't come cheap."

"He's got a job," Mac assured her. "Tell him I'll stop in to see him later this afternoon—bring him something to read."

He could hear the relief in her voice. "He'll like that, Mac. He'll be glad to see you."

"I'll be glad to see him, too. He's a good kid. You take care, Betty."

"You, too. And thanks so much."

When he'd hung up, Mac frowned and brought his hands to his hips. Maybe Jeff could work again today. Though he'd brushed off Betty's concerns, with people coming in for starter plants, ranchers and farmers constantly needing something, and regulars who hated the drive to Flagstaff shopping for dry goods and groceries, they honestly had been rushed lately. If he hadn't talked Amos out of offering movie rentals, too, they'd really be swamped. He looked up to see Terri watching him, a question in her eyes.

"One of the kids who works for us had a riding accident. His horse threw him."

Her pretty brow furrowed. "Is he all right?"

"His mother said he'll be fine. He has a broken leg, though, so he won't be in to work for a while." Releasing a burdened breath, he walked to the screen door. "I'm going down to the house and grab a few books from my bookcase. I'll get your purse while I'm there. In the meantime, would you phone Jeff Delaney and see if he can work again today? His number's in the back of the phone book."

Amos's annoyed voice carried to him from the living room as he prepared to leave. "*I'll* call Jeff! You know, it's a goldarn shame when a man's family thinks he's too old and feeble t' even make a phone call! 'Specially when it concerns his own store, and the man has a phone right beside his goldarn chair!"

"Fine Granddad," Mac called back wearily. "Terri can get you the goldarn number." He glanced at her again and decided from the strained look around her eyes that her headache was getting worse by the moment. "Where's your purse?"

"On the dresser in your bedroom."

"Okay. I'll be right back." He nodded toward the living room where Amos was still muttering. "Better give the phone book to Chuckles before you tackle the dishes, or he'll go on like this all day."

Minutes later Mac was striding through his home and feeling slightly like an intruder. It smelled of her now, fresh and sweet without being cloying. Womanly.

By the time he entered his room and saw her purse and an assortment of pretty bottles on top of his bureau, thoughts he shouldn't be thinking were two-stepping through his mind.

Then he saw the suitcase sticking out from behind his bed.

"What the hell?" he muttered. Crossing to it, he reached down, plucked through the mishmash of clothing stuffed inside, then straightened to stare incredulously through the window at Amos's house. Was *this* why she was acting so strangely? Was she planning to leave without telling them? Sneak out like the proverbial thief in the night?

Anger knotted his gut as Mac grabbed her purse, then went to his living room, snatched several volumes from his bookcase, and started up the tree-lined, grass-and-dirt road to Amos's place, a litany of accusations banging around in his mind.

But by the time he'd tossed the books in the back seat of his Cherokee and walked into the kitchen, his plan of action had changed.

He wouldn't confront her. The last time they'd talked about a suitcase, she'd gotten so angry and defensive they'd barely spoken for days. Some of that awkwardness was still evident in the way they related to each other. He searched his mind. Maybe there was a reason for those clothes being in the suitcase. Storage, possibly. Or maybe they were old clothes she was getting rid of; he hadn't really checked that closely. No, he wouldn't mention the suitcase, but he'd sure as hell keep his eyes peeled and stay watchful.

That worked for ten minutes, then the knot in his gut twisted tighter at the thought of her leaving. For

Amos's sake—only Amos's, he told himself—he had to know if she'd still be here when he returned tonight.

"Any plans today?" he asked, trying to keep the suspicion and mistrust from his voice.

"Just your grandfather's PT this afternoon," she replied in a low tone. "It's an early session. One o'clock."

"Then you'll probably be here when I get back?"

She took a moment to answer. From the look on her face, it was almost as though she knew what he'd seen, how he'd interpreted it, and needed time to form the correct reply.

"Yes," she finally said in that same subdued voice. "I'll be here."

Mac nodded, his stomach relaxing somewhat. But dammit, he doubted her again now, and he knew he'd be finding excuses to call home a few times today— and later, another excuse to check out that suitcase in his bedroom.

Chapter 8

That night Erin was staring in despair at yesterday's headline from the *Spindrift Gazette* when she heard a sharp knock at the door. Blinking back tears, she shut down the computer, pushed away from the desk and hurried into the foyer. With a quick peek through the door's side lights, she unlocked both the inside and outside doors and stepped back.

Mac assessed her suspiciously as he came inside, obviously noting her increased security. Taking off his black Stetson, he laid it on the table in the entryway, then combed his fingers through his hair. "Expecting Jack the Ripper?"

Erin hid a shudder. He didn't know how close he was to the truth. She dredged up a smile. "No, I wasn't expecting anyone so I locked up." Not exactly true, but close. "During our travels, I got used to being cautious."

His dark eyes cooled at the mention of her wanderings. "I hope it's not an imposition."

"Of course not." So was this a visit? "I...put a pot of decaf on a while ago. Would you like some?"

"No, I'll only be here long enough to get a few things from my closet, and ask a favor."

A favor? "What?"

"In a minute," he said, flicking on the light as he entered his room.

Erin watched him open the closet door and remove a sports jacket, dark slacks, two dress shirts and coordinating ties. Every garment he hooked on his finger looked expensive. It had been clear to her from the start, with the money he'd sunk into this home, that he was financially comfortable; she just hadn't realized at the time that those funds had come from an engineering career.

She held her breath when he glanced almost pointedly at the bedroom floor where her suitcase had once lain. Then he closed the closet door, turned out the light and carried his belongings into the hall.

"Going someplace fancy?" she asked, more to make conversation than from a need for information. She knew he'd come to see if the suitcase was still packed and waiting to be carried out, just as she'd known his phone calls this afternoon were merely a way of checking up on her.

"Possibly. A friend phoned to say he'd be flying in for a visit. Shane likes to party hearty, but he also likes eating at five-star restaurants."

"Shane," she repeated, slightly unsettled by the "party hearty" part of the description, and recalling the conversation in Amos's kitchen. "He's the colleague from New Hampshire who wants you to start a new business with him. When's he flying in?''

"Late Saturday night. I'm picking him up in Phoenix early Sunday morning."

Yet Mac had come for his clothes tonight.

His expression darkened. "As for the business… we'll be talking about it, but it probably won't happen. He wants to start too soon."

"You're dragging your feet because of your grandfather."

"Someone has to keep the store going," he replied, but his grim look told Erin he was torn between his wants and his obligations. "That brings me to my second reason for coming down here tonight."

"The favor," she said. Over time, she'd become the person who drove Amos to his appointments instead of sharing the responsibility with Mac, so that couldn't be what he wanted.

"I need some help at the store—just until I find someone to stock shelves and handle the cash register. I figure if you've been a waitress, you've had some experience as a cashier."

A spurt of panic hit her, and suddenly her mind filled with the image she'd just purged from the computer screen—the face of pretty ex-cheerleader Trisha Giles who would never cheer for anything again. Here on Amos's land, she and Christie were reasonably safe; at the store they would be more visible, more at risk—and for a longer period of time than they were at the hospital in Flagstaff.

She shook her head. She couldn't do it. Charles had funds upon funds. His mother had left him well-off, and his keen business savvy had increased his holdings tenfold. He had the means to find them, and if Millie's fears were justified, he could even now be narrowing the field. "I...I can't. Who would take care of your granddad?"

"I phoned his friend Sophie. I told you about her. She said she'd be happy to sit with him."

"But he'd hate that," she blurted. "He's embarrassed by the cane. I'm sure that's why he wouldn't go into the store the other day when you saw us sitting in the van. He doesn't want his customers to see him struggling, let alone a woman he—"

"He'll just have to accept it. Jeff was only able to work until noon today because he had plans, and he can't come in tomorrow or Saturday. It'll just be me and Martin, and I spend most of my time at the feed shed. Will you do it?"

"You can't find another teenager to fill in?"

"I probably can in a day or two, but High Hawk's a small town. It's not as though we keep applications on file. Terri, I need someone right now."

She scrambled for another excuse. "What about your granddad's PT?"

"Tomorrow's only Thursday. I'll probably have someone by Friday. One day. That's all I'm asking."

Her heart pounded, and she felt torn. How could she deny him after all he and Amos done for her and Christie? He'd even given up his home. That had to be worth one day. "All right," she finally answered reluctantly. "But Christie comes with me."

"That's no problem." Mac pulled his hat back on, tugged it low. "I'll clear enough room for her to play and color close to the register. She'll be fine."

Would she? Would either of them ever be fine again?

Mac's gaze shifted from her to his bedroom again,

then cooled. If she were a betting woman, she'd wager that he was waiting for an explanation for that suitcase. There wouldn't be one.

He brought his attention back to her. "I'll pick you up a little before eight-thirty."

"All right," she replied because she had no choice. "We'll be ready."

As she followed him to the door, she found herself remembering the heat of his hands in the pantry this morning and missing them. But his touch hadn't been the intentional touch of a man who wanted a woman. It had simply been a way of keeping her there while he probed again for more answers she couldn't give him.

A different time and place, and things might be different, a small voice whispered, and Erin thought that might be true. But what good did that do either of them today?

"See you in the morning," he said briskly.

"Good night."

Sighing, relocking both doors, Erin returned to the computer. In a minute, the *Gazette* Web page was back up on the monitor, and she was staring again at the sickening headline hovering over last year's high school graduation photo of Trisha Giles.

A lump formed in Erin's throat as she quickly scanned the text below the photo, looking for additional news. But this telling added little to what Millie had shared. Trisha's death had been tentatively ruled accidental, but a full investigation was ongoing— which made Erin think they weren't sure it was an accident at all. Why would she swim alone at night, particularly in cold waters? And if she hadn't been alone, why hadn't her companion called for help when he or she lost sight of Trisha?

Shutting down the computer, she sank against the chair's backrest, tears stinging her eyes. Sweet, giggly, nineteen-year-old Trisha had lived life joyfully and un-afraid, the product of a sleepy Maine town unaccustomed to violence.

But the world was a frightening place, Erin knew. If further investigation pointed to foul play, she had to believe Trisha's death and Charles's manic crusade to get Christie back were connected. They would have to run again, despite her promise to Amos. Figuratively speaking, it would be more difficult to hit a moving target.

Two gold-banded front teeth gleamed from Martin Trumbull's smile as he showed Erin and Christie around the store the next morning. He pointed out the various grocery items they stocked "…for folks who can't abide that drive into Flagstaff." He was a Norman Rockwell painting with his white, wispy hair, pale-blue eyes, rimless bifocals and perennially stooped posture. A long white butcher's apron wrapped his thin frame, with shiny brown pants and wingtips sticking out of the bottom, and a white shirt and blue bow tie poking out the top.

"Now I don't *have* to work, mind you," he said, his voice cracking with age. "I got a nice pension. I do it because I love people. Always have. I'd also never leave Amos and Mac high and dry."

Erin smiled despite the nervous butterflies in her stomach. "You're a good friend, Mr. Trumbull."

"I try to be," he said, preening a little. "And of course working for Amos has its rewards." He ex-

pelled a raspy chuckle and pointed to the two chairs
drawn up against a black potbellied stove, topped by
a checkerboard. ''I whump Amos nearly every time
we play.'' He then led her to the cash register at the
front of the store, explained that it was the new kind
that told a body how much change to give back, and
flipped the sign on the door to Open. Customers began
drifting inside in less than a minute.

She was busy, mostly in spurts, and managed to
smile through the curious looks and questions several
locals threw at her—mainly, who was she and what
was she doing behind Amos's counter?

All the while, though, she kept a tense eye on Christie, who ran back and forth among the aisles, taking
in everything from the penny candy case, to the pickle
and olive barrels sitting near the wooden cashier's
counter, to the doilies crocheted by a local widow, to
the soft drink coolers, nacho bin, and rotisserie with
slowly rotating hot dogs.

For the most part, Perkins' General Store exuded the
innocence of decades past. But Erin still looked closely
at each customer she checked out, fearing she'd see a
man in his thirties with dyed brown hair and sunglasses.

A tall, ruggedly handsome man with similar coloring reappeared just after 2 p.m., but his hair was not
dyed, and he was not wearing sunshades. Looking at
Mac started a familiar quickening in Erin's pulse. She
hadn't seen him since 8:45 this morning when he'd
left them in Martin's capable hands and replaced the
small Temporary Help Wanted sign in the window
with a larger one.

''How's it going?'' he asked.

''Pretty well. It's been busy, but fun.''

"Good. How about lunch? Did you and Christie eat?"

"We had hot dogs, orange soda and potato chips—" she nodded toward the back of the store "—in your lunch room."

Mac glanced around. "Where is she? And where's Martin?"

He did like to ask questions. "Martin's ticketing merchandise, and Christie and Raggedy Ann are napping on the cot in the back room." There was no way in or out of that room besides the painted white door, and Erin made sure she had a clear view of it from the cash register. She caught the tired look in his eyes. "You look like you could use a nap, too."

As Mac brushed off her concern, two gray-haired ladies came inside, chattering about a friend's medical problem. The taller one stopped abruptly, said something Erin couldn't hear, then marched directly to the check-out counter and plunked her purse on top of it.

Both women were dressed in gaily printed short sets and baseball caps. The woman in the red cap—the taller one, who'd commandeered the counter—pulled a small booklet from her purse.

Motioning her blue-capped friend closer, she spoke to Mac, though her interest was clearly on the booklet she was opening. "Good afternoon, Mackenzie. How's Amos doing?"

"Coming right along, Mabel."

"Good, good. This place isn't the same without him." Her eyeglasses hung from a pearl-studded gold chain around her neck; now she slid the stems through her curls and settled the bifocals on her nose. "I hear Sophie's back in the picture."

Erin hid a smile at Mac's dumbfounded look. She'd

only been here five hours and she already knew Everett Hodge was seeing his chiropractor this afternoon, and Mayor Bradshaw's new lady friend was a retired Phoenix stripper. Small-town gossip traveled faster than e-mail.

Mac nodded at the booklet, ignoring the comment about his granddad and Sophie. "What do you have there, Mabel?"

"Reflexology. It's new. Well, new to me, anyway." Chin elevated, she peered through the bottoms of her lenses, flipped through the pages and found what she was looking for. "Ever heard of it?"

"Can't say that I have." Slouching against the counter, he cocked his head to study the drawing of a hand on the page. Erin did the same. It was divided into tiny sections, each one a different color.

"It's sort of like acupressure, but isn't really. You massage points on the hand—or most times, the feet—that lead to troublesome organs. The stimulation gets things working right again." Turning to her friend, she pointed to a white square on the palm. "See, Essie, it's right here."

"It's an awfully small area," Essie fretted.

"Don't worry, we'll find it." Letting her glasses fall to her chest again, Mabel looked up at Mac. "Essie and I are off for a round of golf, then we're going over to fix Clarice Adderly's gall bladder."

"Sounds like witchcraft," he replied with a grin.

Mabel harrumphed and stuffed the book back in her purse. "Don't sell it short. This could be the next great boon to mankind. Might even put Doc Hastings out of business. You got any golf balls left?"

"Third aisle over, near the back of the store."

Erin smiled as the ladies marched off in their Reeboks, charmed by the conversation—but even more charmed by the broad-shouldered man in the chambray shirt who related so easily to everyone. "You stock golf balls?"

"Golf balls, radiator hoses, a pressure cooker or two. General stores sell general merchandise." His dark eyes danced, and Erin was so delighted by his shift in mood she put her forearms on the counter and eased closer when he lowered his voice. "Though, now that I think about it," he continued, "maybe we should be stocking books on reflexology."

"Not a bad idea," she murmured conspiratorially. "It would be a shame to miss the boat on the next great boon to mankind."

Heat flared in her cheeks as Mac tugged her hand from the counter and turned it palm up.

"Wh-what are you doing?"

"Just a little experiment," he replied indifferently. "Before we sink a lot of money into it, we need to be sure it works."

"Mac—"

"Relax. If this is the next great boon to mankind, it shouldn't take long to test."

Erin's nerve endings tingled, and a shivery warmth suffused her as he began to massage her palm, moving his callused index finger over her skin in slow, sensual circles…constantly moving to new areas and repeating the process.

"You can't possibly know what you're doing," she said nervously, glancing around for customers. "You don't have the book."

"That's what you're here for." He caught her gaze and held it. "You tell me which parts of your body are being stimulated. Your chin? Your earlobes? Your…knees?''

Mabel's strident voice carried to them from half an aisle away. ''Stop getting that young woman all flustered, Mackenzie. Essie and I have a three-o'clock tee-off time and we need to check out.''

Erin jerked her hand away, feeling the flush on her face deepen as Mabel thumped her golf balls on the counter. Hers was the knowing look of a grapevine regular who'd stumbled on a major scoop. ''The price is on the bottom, Terri.''

Terri. So much for keeping a low profile. Every detail that could be gleaned about her had probably circulated the second she answered Amos's ad, missing only those few locals who'd questioned her this morning.

''See you in a while,'' Mac said, straightening and pushing away from the counter. ''I need to get back to the feed shed. If you need anything, give a holler for Martin.''

The teasing light was gone from his brown eyes, but the obvious tension seemed less now, though not altogether gone.

''Thanks, I will,'' she said, accepting the correct amount from Mabel. ''See you later.'' Hopefully, when she saw him again, the effects of his reflexology treatment would be gone. Then again, she wouldn't put money on it. She slipped Mabel's golf balls in a bag.

''He's a handful that one,'' Mabel said, studying Erin as the door closed behind Mac. ''Drags his feet with all the women, and there are plenty around who'd like to put a ring through his nose. You know, he had a wife once. Pretty young thing, but she wasn't the type to stay home and darn socks, if you know what I—''

Disturbed by the woman's willingness to gossip about Mac, Erin placed Mabel's bag in her hands and cut off her statement. "Thanks so much. You two have a great afternoon. Oh—and my best wishes to your sick friend.''

Mabel stared, startled. Then she colored, said, "Thank you, dear," and left, with Essie trailing behind her.

It was a relief when Mac returned a half hour later and introduced her to a redheaded, freckle-faced, six-teen-year-old named Dennis McCallin.

"Denny'll be filling in for Jeff until he's well enough to come back to work," Mac told her.

"Great," Erin replied, smiling at the boy and offering up a thankful prayer. Except for Amos's PT in Flagstaff, she and Christie could now stay safely sequestered at the ranch.

Erin was surprised late Saturday afternoon when Mac tapped at the log home's screen door and poked his head inside.

The kitchen was a straight shot from the door, and crossing her arms over her pink knit top, Erin ambled barefooted from the kitchen where she and Christie had just added the pudding to a cream puff cake. She knew that Mac had left the store an hour earlier than their regular three-o'clock closing today, allowing Martin and Denny to lock up. The ferrier was coming to trim the horses' hooves and shoe them, and according to Amos, for some reason known only to God and horse, Gypsy went wild-eyed at the sight of the man. Mac needed to be nearby to calm her.

"Hi," she said, wondering if this was another visit to check for packed suitcases.

"Hi. Have you started dinner yet?"

"No. Not yet."

"Good. I'd like to borrow your daughter. There's a surprise down in the barn that she should see."

"What kind of surprise?" She didn't want Christie around the horses. Charles had insisted that Erin learn to ride a little, but Pike, Gypsy and Jett were unknown entities, and were at least two hands taller than any animal she'd ever ridden. Their size intimidated her.

"Three baby kittens—a pretty small litter, actually. I promised to show them to her when they arrived." He met Erin's eyes. "Maybe you'd like to see them, too. I thought afterward—since you haven't started dinner—that the two of you might like to join me for a meal at the diner."

Still apprehensive about leaving the ranch, Erin declined. From time to time at the store on Thursday, she'd been stressed, half expecting a stranger to show up and try to take Christie away. She wouldn't return to town without a good reason.

"Thanks, but I have chicken breasts thawing. Actually, I'm surprised you're leaving Amos alone."

Mac stepped inside. "He won't be alone. Sophie showed up a few minutes ago. I figured I'd give them some time together, and kill three birds with one stone."

"Three?" He'd mentioned showing Christie the kittens and giving Amos and Sophie some space. "What's the third bird?"

"You," he said quietly. "Things have been tense between us for days. I was hoping we could get past the blowup over that piece of luggage."

Erin felt herself soften. She wanted to put things back on an even keel, too. This not knowing how to act around him was wearing her out. Well, that and the dicey attraction for him that she couldn't seem to curb, no matter what else was going on in her life. Getting rid of some tension had to help a little.

She summoned a smile. "Christie will love seeing the kittens. Just give me a minute to slip on some shoes."

The kittens were tiny bumps of fluff snuggled against their mother's tummy, one a misty gray like its mother, one black, and one tawny colored.

As she and Mac hunkered down to Christie's level and peered through the slatted door of an empty stall, the earthy smell of leather and hay mingled with Mac's scent—a combination of musk and unmistakable male interest. Erin stilled as that familiar heat swirled between them and their gazes locked for an instant. Then she looked away again to murmur to Christie to keep her voice down because she kept insisting she needed to go inside.

It only took a few minutes for the mother cat to tire of their company and drag her little ones to a darker, straw-covered corner.

Christie teared up when Erin concluded the visit, but Mac came up with a distraction.

"We need some good names for the kitties," he said taking Christie's free hand and leading her out into the sunshine and greenery. "What do you think we should call them?"

She thought a minute. "Bobbie?"

Mac chuckled. "Sure. Barbie's a good name. Now we need two more."

Erin loved the way he dealt with Christie, talking with her in a way that Charles never had. Granted, Christie had been more than a year younger then, but the warmth and fun in Mac's interactions with her were poles apart from the constant teaching diatribes from Charles. He'd wanted a prodigy, not a daughter. Perfection, not a work in progress.

Christie broke away and ran to the corral to see the horses, and Mac and Erin followed. Scooping her up, he set her on the top plank.

"I have a riddle for you, Christie."

"What is a rivvle?"

He chuckled. "Maybe I should ask Mommy instead."

"Uh-uh," Erin said. "Mommy's no good at riddles."

"Come on, give it a try. Why don't baby colts sing nursery rhymes?"

Rolling her eyes, she brushed a few wind-tossed strands of hair out of her face. "I don't know. Because they don't know the words?"

"Nope. Because they're a little hoarse."

Erin groaned and shook her head. But though she searched her mind for a better day, she couldn't recall one, especially when he shifted closer and their arms touched. She'd never felt such contentment before, never experienced such a pleasant sense of family.

She was glad when he suggested that she stop at Amos's to meet Sophie before she and Christie went home. On Thursday, when she'd worked at the store, Mac had picked her up at the house, and that evening, dropped them off there. She was eager to put a face to the strong woman she'd heard on Amos's answering machine.

Passing Sophie's flashy turquoise-and-white 1958 Edsel, they climbed the front steps, the sound of elderly chuckles carrying to them through the screen door.

The couple looked up almost guiltily as the three of them walked into the kitchen. Obviously, they hadn't expected visitors.

Amos's faced flushed six different shades of red.

He was sitting in the middle of the room on one of his chrome-and-vinyl chairs, with his pant legs rolled up to his knobby knees and his bare feet ankle-deep in a basin of water. Sophie was bent over him, adding more steaming water from a teakettle. The clean, sweet fragrance of lavender wafted on the air, along with a few other fragrances Erin couldn't identify.

"Don't you say one word," Amos warned darkly as Mac began to smile. Then to Sophie he growled, "That's enough of this silliness. Get me a towel!"

Sophie Cassleback was a sturdy woman with a round face, ruddy complexion and curly, bottle-blond hair. She was also, it seemed, a woman who took no guff from Amos. She dropped the empty metal teakettle, and it clanged and clattered over the linoleum floor.

"Amos Perkins," she said, fists settling on her ample hips, "you didn't have an objection in the world until your grandson walked in."

"Well, I'm objectin' now."

"That's too bad. Your feet are staying right where they are until those herbs have a chance to work. I didn't grow them, dry them and cart them over here so some thankless windbag could tell me to throw them out before they've done their duty!"

Red-faced, Amos muttered the introductions. "Sophie, Terri. Terri, Sophie."

Erin smiled and clasped the hand Sophie extended. "Nice to meet you."

"You, too," the older woman replied, smiling back.

Erin liked her on the spot, recognizing the warmth and honesty in her direct blue eyes. Erin nodded toward the basin where a gauze bag tied with string and fat with herbs, bobbed between Amos's pink feet. "What's in the bag? I can smell the lavender, but I can't quite place the other scents."

Sophie beamed, Amos's mood forgotten for the moment. "You have a good nose! I threw in some comfrey leaves, pennyroyal, rosemary and a little sage. They make a wonderful footbath for achy feet." She sent Amos a dry look. "That is, when a person gives them a chance to work."

Then Sophie's attention shifted to Christie, and while she fussed over her and asked Erin all the usual questions, Erin heard Mac speak to Amos.

"Granddad, if you don't mind, I have some things to do, so I'm cutting out for a few hours."

"Gypsy havin' trouble with her new shoes?" he grumbled from his chair.

"No, but I've been meaning to do something for a while and haven't had the opportunity until now."

"Fine with me, but Sophie's started supper. You gonna be here for it?"

Erin felt a sympathetic twinge. Amos was as uncomfortable looking as she'd ever seen him. She broke into their conversation before Mac had a chance to answer. "No, Mac's eating with Christie and me tonight."

Mac swung a startled look at her, and she smiled.

"Do you like grilled chicken salads? Christie and I've already made dessert."

"Yeah," he replied quietly. "Yeah, I do." Then, seeming to realize his tone and look might've been too intimate, he added more energetically to Amos, "And now I think I'll get Terri out of here before she changes her mind."

"I'll phone you before I leave," Sophie called as the screen door shut behind them.

"Thanks," Mac called back. "You know the number."

Christie tugged on Mac's hand as they descended the steps. "Let's play wif da kitties."

"Sorry, honey," he said, "they're too young yet. But if it's okay with Mommy, we could take a walk and find some pretty flowers for the supper table."

"Sure you want to do that?" Erin cautioned lightly. "The last time you took her for a walk, we barely spoke for three days."

Mac smiled. "Well, I can't see that happening again." Releasing Christie's hand, he ambled closer to her, the sensual warmth in his dark eyes making her shiver. Drawing her into the loose circle of his arms, he kissed her softly. When their lips parted, Erin's knees were weak and her heart was beating wildly. She gazed into his eyes. "What was that all about?"

"That? That was the thing I told Amos I'd been meaning to do for a while," he murmured. "I just thought I'd be doing it a little later."

Keeping her mind on dinner was a near impossibility because she kept reliving that kiss and wanting more.

Erin was setting the table twenty minutes later when there was a knock at the door. Curious, then suddenly prickling with uneasiness because Mac would've come right in, she drew a breath and went to answer it.

Chapter 9

A wonderful warmth enveloped her when she saw the two of them, framed in the screen door. Mac's wry smirk and Christie's giggles made the image of them all the more precious.

With a put-upon sigh, Mac ushered the toddler inside where she stood for her mother's inspection.

Wildflower chains circled their heads, necks and wrists, and single blossoms sprouted from the strings in Christie's sneakers. A collection of golden columbine with three-inch blooms, and Rocky Mountain irises were jammed into the breast pocket of Mac's navy polo shirt, and blue flax sprouted from the buttonholes in the placket front. Any pocket, fold or flap either of them had was crammed with flowers.

Erin brimmed with an emotion she'd thought was forever lost to her, utterly captivated by this big, rugged man who was secure enough in his sexuality to play like a child.

"Cool, huh?" he said, flashing her a V of fingers. "Peace and love, Earth mother."

"Peace and love," she returned. And she was so afraid that peace and love were exactly what she was feeling. No matter how improbable or illogical, no matter that she'd only known him for three weeks, he was slowly taking over her heart. But could he ever feel the same? She knew he desired her. It was in his eyes every time he looked at her, and it had been in his kiss this afternoon, though he'd kept the pressure light.

"You like kids," she said.

"They can be fun."

"Unco Mac said I'n gorgeous!" Christie piped up.

"Uncle Mac is absolutely right."

"Is Unco Mac gorgeous, too?"

"Yes," she said, feeling her toes curl. "Uncle Mac is gorgeous, too."

As Erin followed Christie into the kitchen, Mac fell into step beside her, plucking flowers out of his clothes and gathering them into a bouquet. He placed them in her hands.

"Ever read *Lady Chatterley's Lover?*" he asked with a suggestive grin.

Erin grinned back, knowing the scene he referred to. "When I was sixteen. My hometown librarian refused to let me check the book out, so I found a table and tucked it inside a copy of *Pride and Prejudice*."

"So?" he teased with a pointed nod at the bouquet in her hands.

Erin laughed, enjoying the lighthearted snap and sizzle between them. But she had to step away before they got into trouble. Not that she didn't find the idea intriguing...but the blooms she held were a little large to twine through his chest hair. ''Why don't you two flower children wash up for dinner?'' she said, changing the subject. ''It's just about ready.''

The evening flew by. When Christie went to sleep, Erin carried their iced teas out on the porch, and they sat together on the big pine swing.

Overhead, the ebony sky sparkled with a billion stars, and a steadily growing moon shone brightly.

''Nice night,'' Mac murmured.

''Yes, it is.''

They rocked for a few minutes in silence, then he set their iced tea glasses on the floor of the porch and kissed her. It felt right, expected, like the perfect ending to the perfect day. He kissed her again. And again.

Erin floated with each kiss, her nerve endings alternately vibrating pleasantly and throbbing with anticipation. The fact that he made no move to touch her made her want him all the more. And then he did touch her. Slowly, sensually. While his left hand cupped the back of her head and his slick tongue mated with hers, his right hand skimmed her throat, her breast, her thigh…learning her curves through her clothing… making her heart pound and her breath thready. This was the seduction she'd yearned for since she'd refused him in the kitchen at Amos's house. But tonight it was fitting.

Mac drew back slightly to slip her hair from its ribbon, then slid his fingers through the loosened strands. ''You have beautiful hair,'' he whispered in a husky voice. ''Why do you tie it back?''

''To keep it out of my face?'' she suggested lightly, wanting his kiss again, wanting his hands.

''Well, it's too pretty to hide.'' He grew quiet for a

moment, then said, "Did your husband like it tied back?"

Erin stilled for a beat before she replied, wondering about his timing. "He liked it long and loose when we were alone, but never when we were out." He'd thought it encouraged men to have "impure thoughts" about her—thoughts only her husband should entertain.

Mac took a few moments to digest that tidbit before he spoke again. "I was married, too. For three years."

"What happened?" she asked, then flushed, feeling like a grapevine regular. "I'm sorry. I shouldn't have pried."

"It's okay. I told you my life's an open book. If I didn't want to talk about it, I wouldn't have brought it up."

Why *was* he bringing it up now? Did he feel she needed more information about him before they took the next step? Or was the sharing expected to be reciprocated? *Quid pro quo.*

He kissed her softly again, then gathered her close and nudged the swing into a rhythm. "Her name was Audra, and I was nuts about her. Unfortunately, I went home one day and found out she was nuts about someone else."

Erin was startled, but kept her voice even. "You found her with another man?"

He expelled a short laugh. "No, that would've been a nice, clean cut." The chains of the swing creaked. "I found out when I saw a slip of paper sticking out from under our dresser. It was an old credit card statement that listed two hotels I'd never visited—and I thought *she'd* never visited. For the three years of our marriage, I left all the bills and finances in Audra's hands. She enjoyed it, and it gave her something to do while we were waiting for a baby to show up.''

He reached for his glass, took a sip and offered her some. Erin shook her head, and he put it back on the floor.

"Anyway," he continued, "being the trusting husband I was, I assumed someone had stolen my credit card number and the charges were bogus.''

"But they weren't," Erin guessed.

"Nope. Realized that after a couple of phone calls. Then I found her birth control pills and knew all her talk about wanting a baby was a lie, too.''

"Mac, I'm so sorry.''

"I was, too. For a while. Apparently, she'd hooked up with her old boyfriend while I was working out of state on a dam-construction job, and they decided they never should've called it quits. They're married now. She's pregnant.''

Erin stilled, unsure of what to say. Mac's wife hadn't wanted *his* child, but she was now carrying another man's? What had that done to Mac's soul?

He went on, wryly. "Turns out, I hadn't only been paying for their overnighters, she'd been funneling money to him from our savings account.''

Stunned that anyone could've treated a man like him so horribly and dishonestly, Erin shook her head. "What did you do?''

"Filed for divorce and got the hell out of Dodge. The way I was feeling, if I'd stayed, I would've run them both over with a 'dozer and spent the rest of my life in a New Hampshire prison.''

He'd been joking, but Erin couldn't smile. "Mac, I'm not defending her—what she did was terrible. But is there a chance she did what she did because you traveled so much in your job? You mentioned you'd worked in another state.''

''I don't know. Maybe. But I figured it shouldn't have made a difference if I was gone for a week at a time. I always flew home on the weekends. I even thought it would help the marriage—the old 'absence makes the heart grow fonder' bit. Guess not.''

''Could she have traveled with you?''

''Sure, if she'd wanted to rough it. But Audra liked to be comfortable—five-star hotels and restaurants, never too far from a spa and a manicure.'' He met her eyes. ''How about you? Would you have looked for someone else?''

Meeting his gaze in the darkness, feeling his nearness so acutely, Erin knew she wouldn't have. ''That's a hard question. I hope I would've ended the first relationship before I started the second, but each couple and set of circumstances is unique. That said,'' she continued, recalling his ''gold band and forever'' speech, ''I can see why you're turned off on commitment.''

Mac set the swing in motion again with the toe of his boot. ''I wouldn't say I'm turned off,'' he said after a moment, ''but I am gun-shy. The next time I fall for someone, I'll be damn sure to look behind the smiles and hormones and know who I'm dealing with. What was your situation? Did you love Christie's father?''

That was an easy question to answer. ''I thought so at the time. But I was married to a man who shouldn't be married to anyone. He was cold and brooding, and…'' She stopped before she added abusive, without conscience and cruel.

''Can I ask why you married him? Were you—''

''Pregnant?'' She shook her head. ''No, I met him

at a bad time in my life and wasn't thinking clearly. My mother had died a year earlier, my dad was nowhere around, and I was on the rebound from a two-year relationship I thought would end in 'I do's.' Then he came along, showered me with gifts, said the things I needed to hear. Four weeks later we were married and a minute after that I was pregnant with Christie.''

She laughed shortly recalling Mark's infidelity and their failed engagement. ''You know, I hadn't thought about it in these terms before, but my mother and I weren't very good judges of men. Do you think there's such a thing as a genetic predisposition to picking losers?''

Mac released a breathy laugh. ''I hope not. When did you know you'd made a mistake?''

''Halfway through my pregnancy. I stayed because after Christie was born, he seemed to change. He was happy—absolutely captivated by her.'' She met Mac's gaze. ''Obviously, it didn't last.''

''Sounds like we both made some bad choices along the way.''

Bad? Bad was a major understatement.

''I thought I knew Audra, too. But when the smoke cleared—when she finally dropped the pretense and told me the truth—I realized she'd been damn near leading a double life.'' His voice hardened. ''I can't imagine any woman having the energy to do that, let alone the guts to lie through her teeth every day.''

Suddenly Erin felt sick. Until that instant she'd been denying the similarity between herself and his ex-wife. But *her* lies were justifiable, weren't they? Wasn't it a parent's job to protect the child she loved, no matter what?

A crushing guilt descended on her and, moving out of his arms, she rose to walk to the head of the steps.

Mac followed, talking to her back. "What's wrong?"

"Just…tired," she said. "It's been a long day."

"That's not why you left," he said soberly. "Isn't it time you told me the truth, Terri?"

He knew?

"You know where we're heading," he went on. "If not tonight, tomorrow. If not tomorrow, the next night. But you're still trying to deny that you want it to happen. Just tell me you're not ready yet."

She sighed at the moon, almost disappointed that he didn't know her secret. "All right. I'm not ready yet."

"Thank you. And thank you for listening to me vent."

"You didn't. Considering everything you've been through, I'm surprised you didn't sound angry."

Mac turned her to face him. "Don't make me out to be a saint. I hated what she did. Hell, I hated *her*. No man wants to be made a fool of. But after two years I finally understand that you have to put the bitterness behind you, or you can't heal. The bottom line is I'm through bleeding over her." He tipped her face up to his. "I've moved on. Have you?"

How could she, when she would never draw a calm breath as long as Charles walked this earth?

Erin shook her head. "No." It was the perfect opportunity to back away; he understood the pain of bad choices, and she would always be moving, especially with mystery still surrounding Trisha's death. "No, I haven't," she repeated, gently moving his fingertips from her chin. "I don't know if I ever will."

The treetops were shaggy and black against the dark

sky, and the three-quarters moon slid from behind their lofty branches to touch his high cheekbones and increasingly cool look. "Okay," he replied after a long pause. "I think we're both on the same page now." But he might just as well have said goodbye because it was in his eyes. "Sleep tight, Terri."

Then he was walking away again, leaving before Sophie's call. Erin told herself it was for the best.

He deserved better than another woman who fed him lies at every bend in the road.

The low mood of the previous night was still with Erin on Sunday morning as she dressed Christie and arranged her hair into twin ponytails. But Christie wanted to see the kitties again, so Erin agreed, as long as she promised to be very quiet and not scare the mother cat.

Erin returned her brush to Mac's bureau, wishing they could attend church this morning. With this brand-new distance between her and Mac, and Trisha's death, she could use the comfort she derived from hearing Reverend Henderson's scripture readings and lessons in living. But if Charles's private investigator had picked up their trail—or if he'd sent someone with dyed-brown hair and sunglasses to find her—Charles would have mentioned that she attended church regularly. It was best that they stay away.

"Okay, twerp," she said, taking Christie's hand. "Let's go see Barbie, Cookie and Shells."

Christie chattered nonstop as they walked the road toward Amos's house, then crossed the grass and headed down the sloping dirt lane to the barn. Sophie's Edsel was parked near the house, and the store's old blue truck was pulled up close to an adjacent outbuild-

ing. But Mac's Cherokee was nowhere in sight. A feeling of frustrated longing gripped her, and she wondered where he'd gone, what he was doing at nine
o'clock on a Sunday morning. Then she remembered
he'd planned to pick up his friend Shane at the Phoenix
airport.

Back came the pressing regret and emptiness of last
night.

Why was nothing simple? If she knew they were
safe, knew there was no way Charles or his hired guns
could find them, maybe things could be different.

But she didn't know that. She'd checked the *Gazette*
again on the Internet—even checked other community
newspapers near Spindrift that had an Internet presence
for updates. But there was either nothing new on
Trisha's drowning or no mention of it at all.

Besides, what would Mac say if she did tell him the
truth? He was a meet-the-problem-head-on kind of
man. He'd demand that she go to the police, which
would be useless. What proof did she have that she
and Christie were in danger? No one had heard
Charles's threats but Erin. She couldn't even prove
that the private investigator who'd shown up in Maine
had been working for him, because she didn't know
the man's name. And even if she could connect the
P.I. to Charles, Charles would say he'd hired the man
to make sure the daughter he loved was being well
cared for.

Erin shuddered. And if Mac cared enough for her
and Christie to confront Charles, he could be hurt. She
knew the explosive rage Charles hid from people.
She'd been on the receiving end of it twice.

Guilt clawed at her. She *never* should have stayed
after he'd hurt her the first time, believing his apolo-

gies, believing that things would get better. She should've found the courage to leave him before he'd made Christie clingy and afraid.

"Okay, sweetie," she said, smiling down at her beautiful daughter. "We're here." She nodded at the barn's weathered doors. "Now, what kind of voice are we going to use in there today?"

Cupping a small hand to her mouth, Christie barely whispered, "Quiet."

"Good girl."

The kitties were mewling softly and crawling, eyes closed, over the straw, their little legs still too weak to support them. Erin crouched beside Christie. "Aren't they cute?" she murmured.

Christie's head bobbed.

"Which one is Barbie? Do you know?"

"I fink that one," Christie whispered, pointing to the tawny-colored kitten apart from the rest.

A deep male voice and the low thud of boot heels shattered the morning stillness. "You'll saddle Jett yourself?" Mac repeated with a touch of humor. "Do you even remember which end of the horse to face, city boy?"

His companion's reply was lost in the quick pump of blood to Erin's ears. Whirling from the stall, she rose as they walked toward them.

Mac stopped in his tracks. Then—grudgingly, Erin thought—continued toward her. Electricity streaked between them, reminding her of their own crackling heat on the porch last night.

The stranger, who had to be Shane Garrett, was nearly as tall as Mac, and every bit as lean and muscular in jeans and a western shirt. He had black hair, a confident smile and a way of walking that just missed being a swagger. He was good-looking, and he knew it. The way he smiled and scanned her white knit top and fitted jeans told her he was already interested.

"Terri," Mac said in a businesslike voice, "this is the friend I mentioned—Shane Garrett. Shane, Terri Fletcher, Amos's housekeeper and caregiver."

"Nice to meet you," they both said at the same time, then laughed and clasped hands. He had a nice laugh, Erin decided—and seeing Mac's face dissolve into a scowl, she decided he could take lessons. He was obviously still upset, angry or both. But there was nothing she could do about the way they'd parted. At this point, distance was the best thing for them.

"I understand you're thinking about moving back here," Erin said, turning to Shane.

"Actually, it's firm now. I'll be finishing up a project with the Army Corp of Engineers soon, then coming back here to get things started. Probably within two weeks." He glanced at Mac. "For now, we're taking the horses out before we head up to Walnut Canyon. Well, close to the canyon, anyway."

When she sent a questioning glance Mac's way, he said, "We're going geocaching."

"Whatever that is."

Shane ambled closer, a charming grin in place, and obviously revving up for a charming explanation. "If you type geocaching into an Internet search engine, it'll tell you all about it, but in a nutshell, it's a treasure hunt for adults."

In the barn's dim light, Erin couldn't tell if Shane's eyes were gray or blue, but there was a persuasive glint in them. She knew his type: not a bad guy, but definitely a jump-their-bones-and-kiss-them-goodbye sort.

He'd been too good-looking from birth, and grew up being eye candy for every female over puberty.

So where had all this intuitiveness about men been when Charles was courting her?

With another scowl, Mac stopped his friend before he'd uttered a dozen more words. "I'll tell her all about it later, Slick. If you want to ride before we head for the canyon, we need to get started."

"Now, just wait a second," he returned. "Let's not be too hasty. Maybe Terri'd like to go with us."

"Terri doesn't ride," Mac replied irritably, "and she has a daughter to take care of."

Suddenly impatient with his attitude, Erin snapped, "Who said I don't ride?"

Mac stared coolly. "You ride?"

"A little."

"The day it stormed and you brought the horses in, it didn't look that way to me."

"Why? Because I was concerned that I might be trampled? Do accomplished riders stand their ground instead of getting out of the way?"

Shane's gaze ricocheted between Mac and Erin, then when the silence stretched, he blew out a low breath and addressed Mac. "Well. As I was saying. You and I could ride for a while, then Terri and Christie could go caching with us afterward. You said it didn't appear to be too long a hike, right?" He smiled at Christie. "How about it, sunshine? Want to take a walk with us?"

Christie had been fine with Shane's presence in the barn until he'd spoken directly to her. Now she bolted from the stall and practically scaled Erin's legs to be held.

Settling Christie in her arms, Erin met Mac's agitated look. He couldn't very well tell her to stay home after Shane had extended the invitation.

"Would you like to go along?" he finally asked. "From what I read, the cache is about a mile walk on a decent dirt road, then a short distance into the woods. It'll be a trek for Christie, but I could carry her when she got tired."

Erin shook her head. She was still annoyed with him, but she was through complicating his life. "Thank you, but we have plans." She mustered a smile for Shane, who looked confused. "Nice meeting you. Enjoy your stay, and have a safe flight back."

His sober gaze flicked between her and Mac. "Thanks. It was nice meeting you, too."

As she walked Christie out of the barn, Shane's low words to Mac carried on the straw-and-leather-scented air. "Okay…mind telling me what that was all about?"

Chapter 10

The knee-deep grass was still wet with dew as Mac and Shane walked their horses through the pasture, passing red-coated Herefords and a collection of diving, sailing crows. Cooler overnight temperatures had left pockets of fog lying in some of the depressions, and it rose from there in sun-filtered light and from the creek bed below.

Mac pointed Pike toward the east meadow, thinking it would be a nice ride for Shane since it was already carpeted with wildflowers. He bit down hard, remembering the *Lady Chatterley* conversation he and Terri'd had yesterday. And how damn much he'd *wanted* her to thread those flowers through his chest hair.

"Okay," Shane finally said, "you've been quiet since we left the barn, and I've given you plenty of opportunities to answer me. Now I'm asking again. What's up? You sleeping with her and trying to keep it hush-hush?"

Mac jerked a look at him.

"Well, what am I supposed to think? You sure as hell didn't want me talking to her, and that little back-and-forth deal between the two of you pretty much told me you were more than friends."

Mac's gaze rebounded to the grasses and depressions ahead, watching for holes and burrows that Pike might stumble into. "I don't give a damn if you talk to her. I just don't want you using her. She's not your type."

"No? Whose type is she? Yours?"

Mac scowled. "Just ease up on the Svengali routine. She's a single mother with a lot on her plate."

"Like what?" Shane asked.

Good question.

"Where's she from?"

"Maine."

"Get out," he scoffed. "We've both heard enough New England accents to know—"

It was hard for Mac to keep the irritation from his voice. "I didn't say, 'originally.' That's where she lived last."

"Where's she from originally? The Midwest?"

"I think so." She'd said she grew up in a small town in Illinois, but who knew if that was the truth?

"You don't know?"

Tugging back on the reins, Mac halted his horse to glare at his friend. "You writin' a book?"

Shane lost the easy tone he'd been using. "Look, don't get ticked off. I'm asking because I care. You like her. Maybe more than like her. I know it's none of my business who you get wrapped up with, but after all the crap Audra put you though... Well, one time through a tree shredder should be enough for any man.''

Mac stilled for a moment, then nodded. He and Shane had been friends for years; if he couldn't share his doubts and concerns with him, he couldn't share them with anyone. And suddenly he wanted to get some things off his chest.

"The truth is, I don't know a hell of a lot about her.''

"That was obvious when you didn't know that she rode.''

"Yeah," Mac muttered. He relaxed Pike's reins and gave the chestnut his head.

Shane followed suit. "So what's her story?''

"She was married to a jerk, left him and has been traveling ever since. I get the feeling she and Christie have seen a lot of the country.''

"She running from something? Like joint custody? Which is a crime, I believe.''

"I asked her the day she showed up here, and she said she wasn't running from anything.'' Or, no...Mac thought. She'd just implied that he'd been off the mark. How had she answered? *Afraid I'll take off with the good silver?* "All I know is, there's no love lost there. I don't think it was an amicable divorce, but I can't quite see her breaking the law. My guess is that the father didn't want anything to do with Christie.''

"You could do some checking. She had references, didn't she?''

"Yeah. Supposedly, Amos checked her out and everything was fine.'' But he still hadn't found that slip of paper Amos had jammed back in his pocket that first day—and hadn't been able to get any cooperation in the memory department from Amos.

Mac felt a jolt as something occurred to him. She'd told him the name of the restaurant where she'd worked. Krafty Millie's Café. The town wasn't coming to him, but maybe the restaurant advertised on the Internet. How many Krafty Millies could there be in Maine?

Turning to Shane, he tried to close the conversation. "The bottom line is, what she does is her own business. She's good with Amos, takes him to PT and sees that he does his exercises. She also cooks better than I do and isn't hard to look at. And with the job being temporary and Amos getting better every day, she'll be on her way again in a matter of weeks."

"That's good to hear. I think." Shane waited until they'd ridden a little farther to ask, "So how hot is it between the two of you?"

Mac released a short laugh. For him, molten lava, that's how hot it was. As for her, he had no idea. One minute she had her hands in the hip pockets of his jeans, pulling him into her, the next she was pushing him away.

"Never mind," Shane said when Mac didn't answer. "I think I know. You going to be okay when she takes off?"

"Why wouldn't I be?" Mac asked, and clicked his tongue to Pike. The chestnut eased into a lope, then a run, hooves thudding over the packed earth, the mountain air crisp against Mac's face. "You worry too much," he called over his shoulder. "See you at the creek."

When the horses were cooled down and in the pasture again, Mac and Shane walked up the dirt road to the house and entered through the kitchen door. Mac was startled to see Terri and Sophie carrying platters of pancakes, sausage, scrambled eggs, bacon and toast to the table. Everything looked piping hot and smelled great. The leaf had been added to Amos's maple table, and there were six place settings there instead of the four he'd expected.

"Just in time!" Sophie called happily as she set down her platter, then bustled back to the stove. "We can dig in as soon as I get Amos's oatmeal ready."

Amos yelled from the living room, his nose obviously out of joint again. "I ain't eatin' oatmeal when everybody else is havin' good food!"

"All right," Sophie yelled back, "you can have a small pancake because it's Sunday and you have company. But no bacon or sausage."

With a grin for Mac, Shane glanced around the busy kitchen. "Think I'll go visit with your granddad until Sophie calls us in. I haven't had time to say more than hello to him since I got here."

"Thanks," Mac returned, "he'll like that." Then, bracing himself, he meandered over to the table where Terri was placing silverware on the white paper napkins Christie was carefully laying next to the plates.

"Hi," she murmured, not looking up.

"Hi," he replied in an undertone. "I didn't know you were joining us for brunch."

With a veiled glance at Sophie, she answered just as quietly, "Neither did I. Amos stopped us as we were taking a walk. He said Sophie'd be hurt if we didn't join the four of you. I'm sorry. I know you'd rather we weren't—"

"All right, Your Highness!" Sophie called, carrying Amos's oatmeal to the table. "Time to feed your royal face!"

"'Bout time I got some respect around here," Amos yelled back. A moment later he limped into the kitchen with Shane following behind him.

Hooking his cane on the back of his chair, the old man lowered himself into his seat and patted the chair to his right. "Now you sit down, too," he said to Sophie. "And, Shane, you sit on the other side-a me. I want to hear more about this new business yer gonna open."

That left three seats. Christie's booster chair brought the number to two. Mac ended up seated next to Terri, brushing knees, elbows and libidos with her through the whole meal until he was afraid to stand, and damned annoyed by the whole thing. It was a relief when the meal was over and the kitchen went into busy mode with everyone helping to clear the table and do the dishes.

Amos alone sat sipping a second cup of decaf. "If you boys 're goin' up to the canyon, you oughta be goin' soon."

"I agree," Mac replied.

At the same instant Shane said, "I'll have to pass today."

All heads turned in Shane's direction.

"The truth is," he said apologetically, "I'm beat. I didn't get much sleep last night on the flight, and this mountain air—not to mention your wonderful breakfast, Mrs. Cassleback—has me just about ready for a nap."

Sophie beamed.

Shane glanced at Mac again. "Why don't you take me back to my sister's house so I can crash? Then you can take Terri and Christie caching. We can catch up over dinner on Tuesday."

"Tuesday?" Mac's gaze narrowed. "Thought we were having dinner tomorrow night."

"Sorry, Monday's booked—Sally's cooking. She wants me to meet her latest boyfriend. But I'll be here until Thursday. We'll have time to talk."

Mac dug in his jeans pockets for his keys. "All right, Tuesday it is." Then as Shane said his goodbyes, Mac added that he'd be back in a half hour or so.

He glanced at Terri, though he wasn't sure why. Maybe to see if she cared that he was leaving again. But she looked away, so did he, and then he was out the door.

"Does Sally have a computer?" Mac asked as he and Shane walked to his Cherokee.

"Doesn't everyone?"

"How about an Internet server?"

"Again, doesn't everyone?" Shane climbed into the passenger side, snapped his seat belt, then knocked the seat back and closed his eyes. "Sally lives and breathes for the World Wide Web. I wouldn't say she's a geek, but if she had a poster on her bedroom wall, it would be of Bill Gates, not Brad Pitt." He cracked an eye open. "Planning to surf the information super-highway at my sister's place?"

Mac started the car and pulled out of the driveway. "Damn straight."

When he returned to Amos's place, Mac had a phone number in his shirt pocket, and he was edgy because he wasn't sure what he was going to do with it. Terri and Christie were still there, talking and playing Candy Land with Sophie and Amos. He could see the affection in Amos's eyes as he let Christie draw a card with a colored square and then "help" him advance his game piece to that color. She'd drawn a blue card. Ordinary, everyday blue. Nothing like the deep, hauntingly beautiful cobalt color of Terri's eyes.

Mac called himself a horny idiot and proceeded inside the kitchen. As he hung his car keys on a hook by the door, Sophie looked up from the game.

Never one to mince words, she started in on him immediately. "Amos and I were talking after you left, feeling bad that your plans were spoiled when Shane bailed out on you. We think you should take Terri out to Walnut Canyon."

Mac swung a sharp look at Terri. She was as startled as he was. The two of them spoke at once. "Mac's been up since dawn," she blurted. "He's probably exhausted."

"Who's going to look after Christie?" was Mac's question.

"Sophie and me kin watch the little one," Amos said releasing a rusty chuckle. "And when I was thirty-five, I didn't have no trouble at all stayin' awake when there was a beautiful woman beside me."

Color crept into Terri's cheeks at the compliment, but Mac had another reaction.

Despite his reservations and the phone number in his pocket, his sex drive kicked in, the damn thing already contemplating the trip and the private time they'd have there.

The canyon was beautiful in summer, wildly primitive with Douglas firs, cottonwoods and pines. There wasn't a doubt in his mind that Terri would enjoy seeing the limestone cliff dwellings. But in her own subtle way, she'd made it clear last night that their relationship would never go beyond friendship, so he and his hormones had decided to adopt a cool-it attitude. Well, he had, anyway. His hormones were a little slow on the uptake today.

"Granddad, it's going on two o'clock already, and the monument closes at six."

"You got time. It's only seven miles from Flagstaff."

"But by the time we get there, check out the visitor's center and walk the path, it'll be time to leave. Besides, Terri doesn't like crowds, and it's too late to reserve a spot and a guide for the Ledge Walk."

Erin blinked in irritation. *Terri doesn't like crowds?*

"So, do the Island Walk," Sophie prompted. "It might not be crowded at all. With Amos doing so well, and Terri telling us that she'll be moving on soon, time's growing short. It would be a shame if she left without seeing the cliff dwellings."

"An opportunity like this don't come along for her every day," Amos chimed in. "And she don't need a guide. You been there enough times to tell her everything she needs to know."

"Granddad, please. You're railroading her. Can't you see she doesn't want to go?"

Erin's blood pressure spiked. Once again Mac was making her decisions for her, and Charles had done that too many times in too many ways to put up with it from another man.

"I'd love to go," she said firmly. "Christie and I *will* be leaving soon—sooner than we'd thought. And I'd like very much to see the cliff dwellings. If you don't want to drive me, maybe I'll take Amos and Sophie up on their offer to watch Christie and go myself."

She watched Mac's eyes spark. "You don't understand," he said to her. "It's 185 feet down to the ruins, and there's no elevator for the return trip. You'd be climbing steps both ways. It's a strenuous hike.''

"And I'm what? Too old? An invalid? Grossly out of shape?''

"I didn't say that.''

"Why don't I give Terri directions?'' Amos interrupted with a grin that only added fuel to the fire. "As for babysittin', Christie and me get along fine. I'm your stand-in granddaddy, ain't I, little bit?''

Christie drew another card. "Gween, Aunt Soapie!''

Mac pinned Amos with an exasperated look, then his gaze rebounded to Erin. "Terri, look. It'll take more than a few hours to do it right. We wouldn't be back until after supper.''

But there was more than exasperation in that look, she realized. There was a message. He was telling her that they had unfinished business, and if she knew what was good for her, she'd make her excuses and forget this ridiculous notion.

She knew she should. She knew it with all her heart. But suddenly her mind was weighing the pros and cons. It was doubtful that anyone Charles sent to find her would think to look for her at a tourist hot spot, so she and Mac would be safe there. Also, seeing the cliffs would be a wonderful experience to share if she ever returned to teaching. But it was the third consideration that made her nod her assent. One look at his dark eyes and rugged features, and the promise she'd made to herself became less important than being with him. Her life had been a nightmare for months, and recent events hinted that it would continue to be. She deserved a few hours of happiness.

Erin spoke quietly to Christie. "Honey, if I go for a ride with Uncle Mac, would you be happy here with

Aunt Sophie and Papa Amos? I'd be gone for a long time, so you'd have to take your nap on the couch.'' Which was really no different from what she did during the day when they cared for Amos. ''But I'd be back by bath time to read you a story and tuck you in.''

''Da baby bunny story?''

''Yep, *Little Cottontail.* And maybe we could have ice cream for a bedtime snack tonight instead of cereal.''

''Okay!''

Rising, Erin removed her game piece from the board, then hugged and kissed Christie and murmured for her to be a good girl. She then stared at Mac, who looked as though he were on his way to a hanging and would be deliriously happy to see her neck in the noose next to his. ''I'm ready,'' she said. ''But I'd like to stop at the house first and get my camera.''

The twenty-seven miles to the ruins took very little time because Mac drove like a man possessed—like a man who wanted to just get the whole trip over with. By the time they passed the sign welcoming all to Walnut Canyon National Monument and sped along the access road to the ruins, Erin was feeling the same way.

Her mood changed, however, when they reached the canyon. They skipped touring the pretty stone-and-wood visitor's center snuggled in among the trees in favor of starting their leisurely trek down to the dwellings.

''We can collect all the brochures you want, and check out the exhibits when we come back up,'' he said grimly, leading her past the building and onto a paved trail. "The center should still be open."

Then, there it was.

Erin's first glimpse of the canyon took her breath away. It was vast, formidable, with its steep stone walls, plunging gorge and thick proliferation of trees and scrub pine virtually growing from solid rock.

"Oh, my."

"Yeah," Mac said, still hanging on to his mood. "Hard to imagine people living here, isn't it? Raising kids here had to be tricky." He nodded ahead. "Let's start down."

Mac guided her down the long paths and sets of steps, both of them taking time to drink in the scenery along the way. It was a strange feeling, walking down to the canyon's midlevel with so much open space around her—daunting if not for the pipe railings set by the park service. She kept walking, though, snapping photos and following other tourists down to where the pale, prehistoric ruins waited.

There were twenty-five in all, every one of them a testimony to the resourcefulness of their architects. As they passed, then stopped to peer inside the crumbling walls, Erin decided that it truly was amazing that anyone had called this place home. Mammoth rock outcroppings served as ceilings, with the walls and frontages of the homes built of shaped and plastered limestone, some of the bricks darkened by the fires of the people who'd once lived there. There was an astonishing view of more cliff dwellings on the opposite canyon wall.

Mac spoke like an automaton as they stopped at an overlook, firing off statistics like someone with a travel brochure in his hip pocket.

"There are about three hundred dwellings strung along both walls of the canyon. Some of them were homes and others were used for storage by the tribe."

"Which tribe? Pueblos? Anasazis?"

He raised his eyebrows.

She sent him a dry look. "I taught kindergarten, but I did take more than cutting-and-pasting in college."

Erin waited until a noisy family of four moved past them to speak again, then she did so in an undertone. "Mac, I'm not here because I wanted to spite you in front of your granddad and Sophie. It's just that they were talking about the ruins when we were playing Candy Land with Christie, and while I didn't necessarily need to see it with you, I *was* interested."

She paused. "I just got irritated when you kept answering for me instead of letting *me* tell them I'd rather wait to see it another time. Especially after you did the same thing to me in the barn this morning with Shane."

He sent her a blank look. "I don't know what you're talking about."

"Yes, you do. You answered for me there, too. You assumed I didn't ride or didn't want to ride or go caching with the two of you instead of letting me be the one to say no."

His tight lips parted, and he drew a soft breath. "I'm sorry. I wasn't in the best frame of mind either time."

No kidding, she thought. But then, she hadn't been all sunshine and light, either.

"To answer your question," he said, staring out at the cross-canyon ruins, "the people who lived here were the Sinaguas—which means, literally, 'without water.' It's still in short supply here. Water at the visitor's center has to be pumped from a well two thousand feet deep.''

"Wow."

"Yeah." He finally smiled. "I assume that's true, anyway. I read it in one of the leaflets I got at the center a while ago. As I said, before we leave, we'll stop so you can pick up a few."

They walked slowly, dodging other visitors, peering into several of the dwellings, with Erin snapping photographs inside and out. He motioned to a long rock shelf adjacent to the pathway outside one of the ruins. "Come on. Let's sit for a minute before we go back."

"Are we allowed?"

"Sure. We can do anything we like as long as we don't take or disturb anything here. It's still a sacred place for modern-day Pueblos."

Erin followed him to the rock, and they sat for a time marveling and appreciating. But there was something important missing. Surrounded and immersed in so much natural splendor, his touch would have made the experience better—a way to acknowledge that they were sharing this together, not apart. But that was asking a lot from a man who hadn't wanted to make the trip with her in the first place.

Erin closed her eyes and filled her nostrils with the heady scent of pine, blocking out the voices from the trails above—yet hearing the melodic calls of birds and feeling the warm canyon wind on her face. She tried to imagine a people who farmed this unforgiving land and fashioned pots from red clay...children who raced along the trails playing with dolls made of fur and bits of bone.

She tingled when Mac laced his fingers through hers.

"So what's this about your leaving sooner than you expected?" he asked quietly.

Erin opened her eyes to meet his, sorry that when he'd finally spoken, he'd brought up an unhappy topic. She glanced at the other side of the canyon. Overhead, a trio of turkey vultures skimmed the warm thermals, black against the blue of the sky.

"There really doesn't seem to be any reason for me to stay. "Sophie and Amos are back together, so to speak, and I know she wants to take care of him. What's the old saying? Three's a crowd?" She glanced at him. "I told Amos when I took the job that I'd stay as long as he needed me. He's doing great. Vicki said the other day that they're getting close to discharging him. I'm not needed that much anymore."

"Not necessarily," Mac returned sensibly. "Sophie has obligations, too. She has a son, daughter-in-law and grandkids in Sedona who need her occasionally, so her time isn't completely her own. I don't know who would win—"

He fought a scowl when another group of people passed by, the oldest of the children whining about the long hike back to the top. When they were out of earshot, he continued. "As I was saying, I don't know who would win if there was a tug-of-war of affections. I'd hate to see Amos without a caregiver before he's ready to go solo."

"I would, too."

"So will you stay until he's well enough to go it alone?"

"I made a promise."

"But are you going to keep it?"

Erin searched his dark eyes, trying to see into his thoughts. "Are you asking because you're concerned you might have to line up another housekeeper? Or are you asking for some other reason?'' *Do you care about me? Would you miss me if I left?*

It took a moment for him to answer. Then, quietly he said, ''I'm just asking.''

It wasn't the answer she'd hoped for, and Erin had to hide her disappointment. ''I'll stay as long as he needs me.'' *If I can,* she added silently. Who knew what was ahead for her and Christie?

Mac drew her to her feet. Then with grave uncertainty in his eyes and a look that told her he didn't want to do it, he lowered his mouth onto hers and kissed her. But the kiss was bittersweet. His lips were gentle on hers, seeking, but not plundering, tasting but not taking command. He didn't even hold her, maybe because he was giving her the opportunity to move away.

As if she could. The canyon wind had begun to stir emotions that didn't need stirring.

They only drew away when voices from the trail behind them announced that they would soon have an audience. Mac's expression turned somber again when they'd exchanged hellos with the passing group and the family had trekked off toward the top again.

''I made a promise to you, too,'' he said, his gaze locked with hers. ''I haven't delivered on it yet.''

An involuntary shiver moved through her. ''What promise?''

''The one I made in the barn this morning when Shane was dazzling you.''

Erin shook her head. ''Mac, you're telling me how I feel about things again. Shane wasn't dazzling me. Shane *couldn't* dazzle me.'' Not the way you do with your too-serious looks and simmering sexuality. With your kisses that keep me wanting more, no matter how dangerous they are for both of us. "And I still don't know what promise you're talking about."

Taking her hand, he led her inside a nearby dwelling, deep into the shadows of the cave.

"I told you I'd explain geocaching," he whispered, taking the ribbon from her hair, then combing his fingers through the strands. But they both knew that caching was the furthest thing from his mind.

Erin's breath caught as he wrapped the ribbon around his index finger, then slowly tucked it inside the front pocket of her jeans.

Mac traced the slope of her face with his fingertip, his gaze even more somber than it had been outside. "Cachers hide a container filled with small treasures and post the location on the Internet," he whispered. "Then searchers enter the latitude and longitude of the cache into a GPS, and try to find it."

"Treasures?" Erin whispered, excitement tingling along her nerve endings.

"Simple treasures. A ribbon, a feather, a coin... Do you know what a GPS is, and how it works?"

She could scarcely hear her own voice. "A global...something."

"Global positioning system," Mac rasped, settling his hungry gaze on her mouth.

He bent to kiss her again, their warm breaths melding, their tongues mating...their hands, of their own accord, starting the slow, sensual exploration of lovers. Over shoulders...over arms. Erin trembled as his hands skimmed her sides to her hips. Then his thick fingers hooked through the belt loops of her jeans and fitted her more closely to him.

"Anyway," he whispered as her nerve endings

thrummed and vibrated. "It's a lot of fun, and maybe we should do it sometime." Slowly bringing her hand to his lips, he kissed each of her fingertips, then kissed her palm. His tongue slipped out to taste her skin, and Erin felt her insides turn to silk.

"I'll show you my GPS when we get back. It's small. Only the size of your hand." Then, watching her eyes, he slowly slid her hand down his chest to his belt buckle.

And their world went wild.

Chapter 11

They came to each other in a flood of need.

Mac crushed his mouth hungrily over hers, and Erin kissed him back with total abandon. She opened for his slick tongue, let hers mate with it as it plunged and plundered, taking what it wanted and leaving her quaking and holding on to him for dear life. Blood pounded in her ears as the kisses and touching went on and on, becoming bolder with each passing moment. I deserve this! she told herself, ignoring the strange voice in her mind warning that it was time to leave the park. She would not leave the park. She would stay and she would take what he offered and give him as much back as she was capable of giving.

How she'd missed the heat singing through her blood, the fire licking along her veins. Erin drove her hands through his thick hair, deepening the kiss, frustrated that she couldn't get closer, and fighting the overpowering urge to drop to the clay floor and be his completely.

She felt the cooler air on her skin as Mac yanked her knit top from the waistband of her jeans, then tunneled beneath it to deftly unhook her bra.

Erin tore from the kiss as his callused hand closed on her breast. Her nipple went bullet hard against his palm. ''Not here,'' she said in a trembling murmur. ''It's too public.''

Removing his hand, Mac buried his face in her neck, drizzling kisses onto her throat. He hooked his arm beneath her bottom, then lifted her high to nuzzle moist kisses over her collarbone and the swell of her breasts through the open placket of her shirt.

''Everyone's gone now,'' he rasped, slowly sliding her down his length, then holding her against his arousal. ''The bunch that went by a minute ago was the last of them.''

He captured her mouth again, and Erin gave herself over to his taste and texture and heat for another mind-spinning minute…until clear thought made another gasping comeback.

''But others could come down from the top.''

''Uh-uh. It's too late. The park'll be closing soon. The rangers and SCAs won't let anyone else start the walk.''

''That's exactly right,'' an unfamiliar male voice stated from outside the dwelling. ''We won't let anyone else start down.''

Shocked, Erin and Mac sprang back from each other to gape at the uniformed man on the path.

''And the park's already closed,'' he continued, laughing a little. ''Guess you folks didn't hear the announcement.''

What she'd heard was. an announcement? She'd thought it was a last-ditch warning from her conscience.

Mac's embarrassment gave way to self-deprecating humor. Bringing a hand to his hip, he chuckled softly. "Guess we didn't."

Wishing the floor would swallow her up, Erin spun away to rehook her bra and tuck her shirt back in.

Mac ambled a few steps toward the brighter light of the doorway, his boots scuffing over clay and stone. "Give us a minute, okay?" he asked the ranger. "We'll be right up."

"Sure. Only a minute, though. We can't leave until your vehicle's out of the lot, and we'd like to go home and get some supper. Oh—and don't forget your camera." His parting words carried to them as he walked away, chuckling. "You know, there have to be safer and more comfortable places to make out."

Mortified, Erin met the amusement in Mac's eyes.

"Well. That was fun. I haven't been caught necking with a pretty girl since my high school principal found me with Jacki Elliot in the weeds behind the school."

"It was *not* fun, it was humiliating," she muttered, then peered out from the dwelling to make sure the ranger was far enough ahead of them before she ventured out. Grabbing her camera from the rock ledge, she strode quickly along the paved path.

Mac followed. "Terri, slow down, it's a long way to the top."

"Dear God," she went on, increasing her speed. "I don't know how I could have— I don't *do* things like that."

Mac snared her hand, stopping her in her tracks, and turned her toward him. Draping his forearms over her shoulders, he smiled down into her eyes. "Relax. We didn't do anything wrong. The devil isn't going to take an elevator up from hell and drag us back down with him."

"But I don't do things like that!" she repeated.

He pecked a kiss on her lips, that playful grin still in place. "Maybe I'm just irresistible."

Erin sighed. "Mac, how can you be enjoying this? We're adults. We're supposed to have some self-control. Look at you. Your hair's all over the place, your shirttail's half out and your—" She flushed, seeing that he was still extremely interested in finishing what they'd started.

He wiggled his eyebrows suggestively.

Then, suddenly, it *was* funny, and she had to fight a smile. Maybe he was irresistible. "You're a wreck."

"That would be your fault," he teased, then added, "Your mouth's all red and puffy."

"And that would be your fault." Shaking her head, she reached up to finger comb his thick, dark hair, then pulled her ribbon from her jeans pocket and tied her own into a low ponytail. "Now can we please get out of here?"

"Sure. Want to stop at the center and get those brochures?"

"No!" she shrieked. And their laughter echoed through the canyon.

"I had a nice time this afternoon," he said when he walked her and Christie back to the house.

Though Christie ran inside to put her latest sheaf of crayon drawings on the refrigerator, Erin lingered on the porch. She didn't want the day to end. It had been so long since she'd laughed, enjoyed…felt young and pretty and desirable.

"I had a nice time, too," she admitted, smiling sheepishly. "All things considered." Mac had collected Christie on his own when she'd checked her reflection in the Cherokee's visor mirror and discovered just how red and whisker burned her chin really was. "It's a beautiful place. I'd love to go back and take the Ledge Walk sometime."

"Maybe pick up those brochures?"

"Maybe," she repeated, smiling again.

Mac's gaze softened. "How about next weekend? I could make reservations."

Erin hesitated. Though she desperately wanted to, she couldn't say yes. She didn't know what she'd be doing next week…or where she would be. "We'll see," she replied, then briefly glanced at the door behind her when Christie squealed that she needed help. "Sounds like she's having a tough time hanging forty pictures with six magnets. I'd better go in."

Mac nodded, a message in his eyes that made her heart swell again. Stepping closer, he kissed her gently, no grinding pressure this time. "Sorry about your chin," he murmured, then smiled. "I'll take a razor along next time."

She smiled back, hoping there could *be* a next time.

Then he descended the steps, too handsome and wonderful and decent and understanding. Because he hadn't suggested returning to the house after Christie was asleep…perhaps waiting for her to extend the invitation. "Good night, Mac."

"Good night." Midway to his SUV, he turned and

grinned again. "By the way, if you need anything—anything at all—call me. But don't use the intercom. Amos will hear."

Would she spend the rest of her life regretting? Erin wondered later as she tucked Christie in for the night. After fixing herself a cup of tea, she dropped into a kitchen chair and stared at the camera that held her memories, sitting on the oak table. *Mac's* table. Mac's chair, Mac's home, Mac's everything. And yet…he was bunking at Amos's while she and Christie slept here, taking advantage of his generosity.

She was falling in love with him. The realization was bittersweet, but it still sent a sweeping thrill of excitement through her. Had she ever been in love before? She didn't think so. Nothing she'd ever experienced compared to this mixture of elation at his touch, and futility that she would soon have to give it up.

Still…

Erin jumped up from the table and went to the computer room, charged with the knowledge that she could love again, that she could even be *open* to love after Charles. She had to tell Lynn. Excitement bubbling in her veins, she booted up the computer and started writing an e-mail.

Dear Lynn
How are you? I miss you! Especially tonight when I have so much to tell you and thank you for, because without your help, I might not have had the courage to leave.

She started typing Christie's name, then experienced a jolt of paranoia and deleted it, even though the ''sender'' box on Lynn's computer screen would indicate that the e-mail was from M. Corbett.

> We're well. I won't tell you where we are, but we're safe and happy. Lynn, I've met a man. He's everything I've ever wanted and dreamed of— strong and good and solid and so downright sexy my lungs shut down every time he looks at me. I know, I know. You think it's just hormones because of the way you and Al crashed and burned after the wedding, but I swear, this is real.

It was the longest and most cautious e-mail she'd ever written, but she couldn't seem to stop herself. She didn't name the park, but she had to tell Lynn about their trip to the cliff dwellings, and about her embarrassment when the ranger found them together. But mostly she needed to share the unique and boundless joy she'd been feeling since then.

> I don't know where this will go, if anywhere. It's still dangerous for me to plan a future, especially in light of certain recent events. Also, I don't know how he feels about me. But Lynn, I want to stay. It feels right here.
> All my love and gratitude to you and Jeremy.

Smiling, Erin pushed the send button.

The next morning Erin was crouched beside Christie in the laundry room adjoining the new bath, watching her daughter sort light clothes from darks when Amos came to the doorway.

Christie glanced up happily, her little face wreathed in smiles. "I'n helping, Papa Amos!"

"You sure enough are, honey," he said with a grin, giving her black ponytail an affectionate tug.

Erin smiled, too. He'd been quiet all morning, obviously stewing about something, and she thought his silence might be about Sophie, who hadn't yet phoned or come by. "What's up?"

"Nothin' important, but…" He worked up a frown and a gruff voice. "I been worryin' about my store. I think I should take a look at what the boy's been doin' with it." He hesitated, seeming to gauge her reaction, then went on in the same, obviously contrived tone. "There's some things you gotta do if yer gonna have a decent business. Like puttin' some items in the front of the store to catch a body's attention, and buryin' others in the back till the calendar says it's time to bring 'em out."

Erin pushed to her feet, pleased that he was finally ready to swallow his pride and visit his store. Although, over the past few days, she'd noticed that his cane had become more of a decoration than a necessity, so maybe there wouldn't be much pride to swallow.

"Good idea," she declared. "After all, Mac isn't exactly a retailer, is he? Would you like to go tomorrow afternoon? Either before or after your PT session?"

Amos frowned again. "Well, I wouldn't mind goin' today. That is, if you can get away from the wash and all."

"I can do the laundry anytime," she answered, tamping down her uneasiness at going to town again. This was too important a step for Amos to let fear shut it down. "In fact," she added, her heart doing a silly stutter step as she pulled the ribbon from her hair, "we can leave right now. Just give me a minute to find Christie's sneakers."

It didn't take long for nearby locals to hear that Amos was back. Soon, at least a half dozen of them had stopped by to join his customers in shaking his hand and telling him how good he looked. Erin hung back, watching from the fringes as Amos beamed from the attention. She still felt vulnerable, particularly when a stranger with brown hair and a mustache came inside and asked Martin for directions to Sedona. But coming here was the right decision. She was even more certain of that when Mac came up from the feed shed, met her eyes, and smiled his gratitude.

When the store had cleared, and Amos and Martin had cozied up to the potbellied stove and the checkerboard, Erin moved closer to watch. Christie had already attached herself to "Papa Amos's" side, and was happily holding the checkers Amos won from Martin.

She felt Mac's presence behind her before he touched her. All the signals were there. The tiny prickling of the hair on her arms, the excited tingle…the faintly breathless feeling of falling but knowing she'd land safely.

His hand slipped into hers and lightly squeezed. She squeezed back. And suddenly Erin realized they'd come to a crossroad—and an understanding. Maybe she'd known it since yesterday.

Without a word to the checker players, Mac led her into the cluttered back room, shut the door and drew her into his arms.

His kiss was soft but long and thoroughly knee wobbling, only a hint of searching tongue. When he eased away, he did it slowly, letting their lips cling a little, letting their breaths mingle, keeping their bodies close. "Hi," he whispered.

"Hi," she whispered back, her heart beating fast. "Amos said he wanted to check on your shopkeeping skills today. See if you were doing everything right."

"I'm glad. But we both know he's really here to show everyone that he's getting better." Then he sighed and tipped his forehead to hers, the reason for that sigh evident when he linked his hands at the back of her waist and brought their lower bodies close.

She could empathize.

"The last thing in the world I want to do is pressure you," he murmured. "But I need to tell you a secret."

She waited.

"Every time I see you I want to sink inside you and stay there for a week. You're all I've been able to think about since our trip to the canyon yesterday."

Warm shivers chased over her limbs. "I've been thinking about you, too," she replied in the same hushed tone.

"And...wanting?"

"Yes." There was no point in denying the patently obvious. Her stomach was a needy knot, and her breasts felt heavy and full. But they had to talk before they made love. It would only be one night—that's all she could commit to right now—but he needed to know what he was getting into before they took that step. Still, the prospect frightened her because she didn't want to look weak in his eyes.

"Christie won't get a nap today, so she'll be out like a light by eight-thirty. I'll be waiting for you."

Then his lips were on hers again, and Erin's heart

was banging double-time when he finally eased away, fear the last thing on her mind.

"Don't do any cleaning when you get back," he groaned when they parted. "Don't even cook supper. I'll bring home something from the diner."

"Why?"

"Because if you're too tired tonight, I'll be dropping ice cubes into my shorts and looking for asbestos underwear."

Erin laughed softly, loving him so much it was impossible to grasp. "Supper's already cooking in the Crock-Pot—and I cleaned on Friday."

"Hallelujah," he breathed. "Wait here a minute."

She watched curiously as he crossed to one of the huge cartons stacked near the cot, then returned with several four-packs of toilet tissue and piled them in her arms.

She raised her brows in question.

"We have to make this look good," Mac said. "We've been in here too long." Grabbing a full carton of paper towels, he nodded for Erin to precede him through the door.

Martin and Amos were staring from their folding chairs when they emerged, both of them wearing knowing grins.

"Stocking the paper aisle, are we?" Amos called, helping Christie slide off his lap.

"Yep," Mac replied carelessly, again nodding Erin on ahead of him. "C'mon, Christie," he added. "You can help, too."

But when they were out of sight, with Amos and Martin's low laughter rolling behind them, Mac smiled at her again and mouthed, *Tonight.*

* * *

Charles set his feet, lined the ball up with the cup, then deftly tapped it with his putter. It rolled across his office floor and into the cup, the mechanism inside instantly popping it out and rolling the ball back to him. He smiled. He would crush whoever he was partnered with this afternoon.

His secretary buzzed him.

Frowning, he crossed to his desk and depressed the intercom. "What is it, Marian?"

"Phone call for you, sir. A Mr. Smith. He said he wanted some advice on one of his mutual funds, but I'm not familiar with—"

Charles's pulse jumped and he was instantly on edge. "Thank you, I'll take it." He lifted the receiver to his ear. "Charles Fallon."

"And you know who I am," came the reply.

"I believe we had an understanding. You were only to contact me about your funds after hours. Does this mean you're ready to sell?"

"Not quite. I just thought you'd appreciate a call before I took off again."

"Where are you headed, Mr. Smith?"

"West. Is this phone secure?"

"Just a minute." Setting the receiver down, Charles walked briskly to the door, opened it and said to his secretary, "I need three copies of the Harrison-White prospectus and an up-to-the-minute position on everything in their portfolio."

The woman was already moving. "Yes, sir."

Back in his office, he spoke into the phone. "You said 'west.' She's heading for San Diego, isn't she? I told you she'd go to her father."

"Maybe, but I don't think so. She's somewhere in

the desert Southwest right now—Arizona, from the description of the landscape she gave her friend, Lynn. According to an e-mail she sent her—''

Charles's blood pumped. ''You can access Lynn's e-mail remotely?''

Smith expelled a laugh. ''Anything's possible if you have a laptop with a modem and a password—which I lifted from her apartment before I left Chicago. To bring you up to date, your ex-wife's working as a housekeeper for some old coot who had a stroke. And here's another news flash. She wasn't interested in the shop owner she met in Maine, but she's shacked up with the old coot's grandson.''

Rage so fierce that it stopped his breath burned up Charles's throat, scorched his face and eyes. He clenched the receiver. ''You're certain?'' he asked hoarsely.

''If not, she's close. She told her friend this guy's the real deal.''

Charles's voice erupted in a rasp. ''Kill them both!''

''I was hoping you'd say that. It won't be a freebie. The price'll be the same for him. Of course, since they're together, you won't have double the expenses.''

''Just do it.''

''My pleasure. Also, you might want to start packing for your flight. It'll probably be Phoenix—and it'll probably be soon.''

''Don't call me here again. Use the private number I gave you when you phoned from Bangor.''

''Fine. I'll be in touch.''

Charles hung up the phone, his hands shaking, his face and eyes scalding. He wanted her dead! *Dead!* In the ground where she couldn't humiliate him anymore!

Snatching up his putter, he strode to the aquarium

and swung hard and fast. The tank exploded in a frenzy of glass, fish and water, surging to the floor, splashing his trousers and shoes.

For a few quiet moments, Charles watched his bright, pretty angels flopping on the soiled carpet, dark purple now where the water pooled. Then, feeling better, feeling confident that his desires would be carried out, he placed the putter in a corner, dried his hands on his handkerchief and opened his door.

Standing stone still beside the copy machine in the anteroom near her desk, Marian Crenshaw met his gaze, her face pale.

"There's been a small accident with the aquarium, Marian," Charles said smoothly. "Get maintenance up here, please. Tell them to bring a bucket and mop."

That evening Erin's nerve endings were so wired and her heartbeat so erratic she couldn't clean up the kitchen fast enough. In fact, there was so much electricity in the air between her and Mac she was certain Amos would either pick up on it or keel over from the sheer power of it. She was close to doing that herself.

Once when she went inside the pantry, Mac followed for a fast, wet kiss, and without a second thought she followed his lead, her nervous hands performing a body-skimming prelude of what was to come. Then she shooed him back into the kitchen again.

They left Amos's house at the same time. Mac tended to the stock and she got Christie bathed and ready for bed. It was nearly seven-thirty when she tossed Christie's Barbie sleeping bag and pillow on the floor in front of the TV in the great room and put a *Barney* video into Mac's VCR.

''Mommy needs to take a quick shower, honey. You watch Barney until I come back out, okay?''

Christie looked up at her, her eyelids already droopy. ''Okay, Mommy.''

Five minutes later when Erin returned with her wet hair in a towel and wearing her white terry robe, Christie was fast asleep. Smiling, kissing her softly, she picked her up, put her in her own bed and went to get ready for Mac.

Thoroughly frustrated, Mac left the living room and strode into the kitchen to rinse his coffee mug. ''No, I don't think it's a good idea,'' he called back to Amos. ''It's a lousy idea. You're not ready for that yet.''

Loaded for bear, Amos came cane tapping into the kitchen after him. ''You ain't my keeper. If I decide I'm gonna do it, you can't stop me.''

Mac brought a hand to his forehead where a killer headache was brewing. This was supposed to be his night for a trip to heaven, and he was slowly but surely being cast into hell. ''Look,'' he said, trying for a calmer tack. ''I know you did well today at the store. But visiting and working are two different things. You still tire easily.''

Amos shot daggers at him. ''Which is why I suggested workin' *half* days.''

''Did you discuss this with your therapist?''

''No, I discussed it with myself, and we both decided it was time I went back to work. Folks've been shoulderin' my responsibilities too long now. Martin's older'n me. His life should be easier.''

''Is that what this is all about? You're afraid Martin's getting worn-out? Because he's not. I only schedule him four days a week, and he mostly runs the cash register.''

Amos got him where he lived. ''You afraid if I go back t'work, Terri'll leave?''

A nerve leaped in Mac's jaw. ''This has nothing to do with Terri.''

''Don't it? I see the two of you together—see you gettin' close. And that's okay,'' he added. ''If the Lord made anything sweeter'n her, He kept it fer Himself. But I need t' feel productive again.''

''It's too soon, Granddad.''

Amos glared at him. ''It *ain't* too soon!'' Throwing his cane on the floor, he stalked back into the living room, then continued into the ''good parlor'' that had been converted to his temporary bedroom after his stroke. ''I'm takin' my life back, boy!'' he shouted, yanking the vinyl bifold door shut. ''If you don't like it, you kin make tracks!''

Frustrated and hurt, Mac strode after him, then stopped at the closed door. There was no lock on it, but he wouldn't take away his grandfather's privacy. ''Granddad, I'm not saying these things to be a hard-ass. I just don't want you to go back and undo everything you've accomplished so far. You haven't even been discharged from PT yet.''

Nothing. Not one word from the other side of the door, though Mac could hear pages being turned in a magazine.

''What if some kid comes racing through the aisles and knocks you over?'' he asked, trying again. ''Or you lift something you shouldn't? I just... You're all I have, and I care.''

Still nothing.

Mac got mad all over again. ''All right, have it your

way. I'm going down to the house to check my e-mail. If you need me, that's where I'll be. But I'm *not* leaving. We need to discuss this again—calmly and rationally. There has to be a compromise somewhere.''

Mac started away, then sighed and ambled back to the closed door. ''Granddad, at least tell me that you heard me. Granddad?''

Chapter 12

The moment Erin opened the door to him and he stepped inside, she could see that something had changed radically. There was no light in his eyes, no warm look of anticipation on his face.

"What's wrong?" she asked, instantly concerned.

"Amos." Mac took off his Stetson and laid it on the table in the foyer, then they both gravitated to the kitchen. He dropped into a chair. "He's got a major bug up— He says he's going back to work."

Erin froze for a second, then took a chair across from him. "Oh. He *is* doing well, but he still has some limitations. What did you tell him?"

"I said it was too soon, and after a lot of yelling, he basically told me that's the way it was going to be, and if I didn't like it, I could get out."

Erin covered his hand and squeezed. "How did you leave it with him? Is he all right?"

"No, he's holed up in his room, and he's barely talking to me."

"But he knows where you are if he needs you?"

Mac nodded, then expelled a pent-up blast of air and walked to the coffeemaker on the counter. It was empty and she felt as if she'd let him down.

"I'm sorry, I didn't make any," she said, her cheeks warming. "I…didn't think we'd be drinking coffee. It'll only take a minute to make a pot."

"No, don't do that."

"I have juice, iced tea and bottled water," she offered, opening the refrigerator.

"Thanks. Water's good."

When she'd handed it to him, he screwed off the lid and took several long swallows, walked around, then took her hand and led her into the living room to the sofa. He only sat a moment before he had to walk again.

"Cute," he said, scanning the framed photos of Christie at various ages lining his mantel.

Erin tensed when he picked up a photograph that showed Christie at a park feeding pigeons, part of the city skyline in the distance.

"Where was this taken?" he asked.

"Chicago," she replied hesitantly. "We lived there for a while."

He stared at her for a long moment, more unasked questions in his eyes. Then he frowned, put the photo back and continued to prowl the room, drinking from the bottle, obviously trying to work through his tension. "The house looks nice," he eventually said, his gaze drifting over the throw pillows, candles and dried flower arrangements then back to the photos on the mantel. "I never got into decorating."

Erin felt her heart constrict. Much as she wanted him to stay, she had to send him away. "Mac you don't really want to be here. Go back to the house. Talk this out with your grandfather. I know he didn't mean what he said."

"I know that, too," he replied. Mac came back to her, set the bottle on the coffee table, then settled in a corner of the sofa and drew her into his arms. It felt wonderful to Erin, even in his present state of upheaval. She'd been waiting for this all day. But she knew he wasn't as focused on the contact as she was.

"I'm just having a hard time with this role-reversal thing tonight. Amos was my whole world after my parents died. He was hurting then, too—he'd lost the daughter he loved, and a son-in-law who'd always been more like a son. But he was strong then, and he showed *me* how to be strong. Now I'm the one making decisions and saying things like, 'This is for your own good.'"

"He's still strong," Erin said firmly. "Weak men don't butt heads with grandsons who are bigger, taller and younger than they are. Amos is one of the strongest men I've ever known, and he loves you as much as you love him."

Trying to coax a smile from him, she met his serious gaze. "You should have seen the pride in his eyes the day I arrived, when you came thundering up the road in that old blue truck. He said, 'That's Mac, my daughter Jessie's boy.' And he didn't have to say another word to let me know how he felt about you."

Reluctantly easing out of his arms, she stood and took his hands, tugging a little until he stood, too. "Go. Take care of this. I'll see you in the morning."

He didn't even ask if she was sure that was what she wanted. He simply kissed her softly and left.

When Mac got back to the house, it was all lit up. Hanging his hat on a peg in the entryway, he walked into the kitchen. Amos was sitting at the table, a lamp from the living room in the middle of it for more illumination. He was wearing his glasses and making out checks for the small stack of vendor invoices Mac had brought home from the store.

"I see you found the bills," he said, feeling his way into the conversation.

Amos glared belligerently, almost daring him to take over. "You got a problem with me doin' this?"

"Not at all," Mac replied, feigning indifference. "I'm glad for the help. In fact, I have another bill upstairs in my room. I'll get it for you." He stopped halfway into the stairwell. "You got a problem with me sleeping here tonight?"

He echoed Mac's reply. "Not at all." But his brittle tone had softened. Amos cleared his throat, keeping his eyes on his checkbook. "You want some cocoa? I know it's summer 'n all, but it just feels like a cocoa night. Been a while."

A sudden pang of nostalgia tightened Mac's chest. "Yeah, it has been a while. Cocoa sounds good." He started back from the stairwell. "I'll get it."

Amos grunted to his feet. "Nah, you go git that bill. I'll fix yer cocoa."

Mac watched through an unfamiliar glaze as Amos limped to the cupboard for two cups and two packets of cocoa mix, then poured hot water from an already-simmering teakettle over the powder and stirred.

Years ago there'd been cocoa-and-toast breakfasts

with his granddad before the school bus came...then cocoa "peace offerings" that had somehow managed to smooth over their growing-pains arguments. He'd forgotten about them. But Amos hadn't.

Amos frowned. "You gonna git that bill?"

"Yeah," he said, his throat now as tight as his chest. "I'll be right back."

And when he returned, they would talk about his grandfather coming in to work for a few hours a week.

Erin lay in the darkness staring at the ceiling and feeling Mac's absence so acutely she wanted to cry. Through the screen in the bedroom window, a coyote called somewhere, sounding as lonely as she was. What was it people said? Oh, yes. Man plans, God laughs.

The even breathing coming from the baby monitor on the dresser changed for an instant as Christie mumbled something in her sleep. Then her toddler's light snores resumed, and Erin immersed herself in regret again.

She'd showered and changed the sheets, left the window open to the fragrant night air...fixed her hair the way he liked it and applied a touch of mascara to her eyelashes. And it had all been for nothing.

All she'd wanted was one night with him. Just one night. Now...who knew if it would ever happen?

Erin gave a start as stealthy footsteps sounded on the wraparound porch. She vaulted to a seated position, instantly sorry that she'd left the window open. Then she heard Mac's low whisper at the screen and her pulse quickened.

"Terri, it's me."

Erin flew out of bed and shoved the long window

high, then did the same with the screen. She was so startled to see him she didn't even ask why he hadn't come to the door.

It amazed her that a man so tall and broad through the shoulders could ease himself through the opening so effortlessly. A shiver of awareness rushed through her as he straightened, outlined by the full moon. He filled the room, dominated it. Her nerve endings curled, and her skin beneath her light cotton nightgown prickled. "Is Amos all right?" she whispered, praying it was so.

"Amos is fine," he whispered back, hauling her into his arms, "but I'm not. I tried to sleep after he turned in for the night, but...I need you."

And she needed him.

Swept away. She was swept away by the sheer power of him and the wild and reckless feelings pumping through her blood.

Mac covered her mouth with his own, kissing her with the passion of a man staking his claim, slaking his thirst for her. Erin trembled as he rained more kisses over her throat and his eager hands moved over her loose cotton gown, finding nothing beneath it. He skimmed her breasts, her sides, her hips, her thighs. Then kissing wasn't enough and the nightie was an encumbrance; he pulled it over her head and dropped it on the floor.

With shaky fingers, Erin reached for his shirt to free his buttons. Finding it already open, she spread her hands through his crisp, dark chest hair, marveling at the smooth, taut muscles beneath, reveling in his shower-fresh scent. She pushed the shirt off his shoulders and arms and it joined her nightie on the floor. Mac crushed her to him, flattening her breasts against his chest as they continued to kiss mindlessly, leaving instinct to direct their hands and mouths.

She reached for his belt, but he wasn't wearing one, dispensed with the button at the waistband of his jeans and felt nothing but soft tapering hair arrowing down from his navel. "No underwear?" she whispered excitedly.

Mac spoke against the rapid pulse in her neck. "I would've come to you naked if I was sure Amos wouldn't be waiting up for me when I got back."

In one fluid motion he lifted her into his arms and carried her to the bed, then laid her down and stretched out beside her, his mouth covering hers again. His hands and fingers caressed her in a way she'd never been touched before, each new foray tender yet spine tingling, gentle yet exciting, familiar yet mind-bendingly delicious. She smoothed her hands over his broad shoulders and down his arms, eager to lavish the same gifts on him.

Easing away, Mac stood and pulled off his boots and she heard them thud to the floor—heard his zipper come down. Then in the silvery glow of moonlight, she watched as he closed the bedroom door, dispensed with his jeans and slid onto the bed beside her again. He was sleek male perfection from his thick hair and rugged face to his powerful shoulders and chest, to his lean hips and corded thighs.

She was an experienced woman; she'd been married, had had a child. But suddenly she felt like a virgin, impatient to know what loving was all about. Because while she'd had sex, she'd gradually come to know that she'd never really made love with a man.

Mac kissed her again, and Erin gave herself over to him fully, his hands stroking and coaxing responses from her she'd never dreamed possible, his talented lips and darting tongue turning kissing into a new intimacy, then carrying those kisses down her breasts to her rib cage and navel. As she did for him. It was as though they'd been destined to be together like this from the dawn of time.

"Are you on the pill?" he whispered raggedly when it became clear that he was more than ready.

"No, there was no need...until you. But it's a safe time."

"Uh-uh," he returned, "too chancy. I brought something with me." He moved away for a moment, then the mattress dipped beneath his weight again as he returned and hovered over her. Then in one smooth motion, he buried himself in her warmth and the dance began...the sleek rhythm began...and the tingling and trembling began.

Erin slid her arms around his neck, her hands in his hair, and drew him down for another deep, deep kiss. Her senses reeled. Reality blurred into breathless fantasy. And suddenly they were at the canyon again, locked together and floating up, up on those warm thermals, leaving the pinions and cottonwoods and dwellings far beneath them. He took her to the sun, and she melted and shuddered in his warmth, then, holding fast to him, she tumbled to the bottom, a breathless freefall that barely ended before he floated her airlessly to the top again. It was a magic ride that turned her limbs to butter, and still he prolonged her pleasure, coaxing yet another response from her. Then the thudding in his blood could no longer be denied, and Erin held him fast, so in love she could barely breathe from the sheer wonder of it...as he emptied himself in a shuddering release and softly groaned her name.

Terri.

Seconds ticked by while Erin held him close to her heart, stroking his smooth back as they both struggled to bring their breathing under control. The jubilation she'd felt a moment ago had faded a little when he'd called her by a name that wasn't hers. Suddenly she longed to tell him everything, longed to have him murmur *her* name. But honesty would spoil this moment and she would not give it up. This tender aftermath was for whispers in the dark, for touching and holding.

Mac eased up on an elbow to kiss her softly, then drew the tangled sheet up over her. With a groggy smile he tucked it around her the way she tucked Christie in at night. "I'll be right back. Don't run away."

"I couldn't if I wanted to," she said through a husky laugh.

"Good."

Erin watched him amble into the master bath, beautiful in his moonstruck nakedness, while tiny aftershocks and tingles of passion still worked their way through her system. She would remember this night as long as she lived. For once, she had been loved. Nothing had prepared her for Mac's unselfishness and caring and exquisite tenderness. No, she would never forget this night.

Clicking off the bathroom light, he came back to her and slid under the sheet to gather her close. "Okay?" he murmured, settling her head on his shoulder and kissing her hair.

"Much better than okay," she replied, trying to ignore the guilt she felt for continuing to live this lie.

But selfish or not, she wanted these few precious moments with him before she told him the truth. Wanted the wonder of lying here in his arms feeling warm and safe and whole and cherished.

I'll know if you betray me, Erin.

A shudder racked through her. Mac jerked his head up in concern. "Terri? What's wrong?"

"Nothing."

"Nothing?"

"No, I—I just got a chill. I'm all right."

"Just a chill," he repeated quietly, and she heard his voice cool a notch. He released an impatient breath. "All right, it was just a chill."

Erin lay there stiffly as Mac settled his head back on the pillow, the mellow mood broken. It was several moments before he spoke again. "You know…it's been obvious from the start that something's going on with you. But if you won't tell me what it is, I can't help you. And I *want* to help."

Erin shook her head against his shoulder. He couldn't help her; helping her could put him in jeopardy, and she couldn't have that. She also couldn't put him off forever without at least admitting there was a problem.

"You're right," she returned, swallowing. "There is something. But please…don't press me about it. Can we just have this time together and forget about everything else for a while? Please, Mac."

She was still in his arms, but with every breath she took, Erin felt him slip further away from her, and it made her ache. In the ensuing silence, Christie's soft baby breathing from the monitor sounded thunderous.

Mac slid his arm out from under her head, rolled to a seated position on the bed and reached for his jeans.

Impossibly, Erin's spirits dipped even lower. "You're angry."

He sent her a forced smile as he stood, then pulled up his jeans and zipped them. "No, I'm hungry. I'm going out to the kitchen."

"The kitchen?"

"Mmm-hmm. Do you like scrambled eggs?"

Fragile as tissue paper, that feeling of being cherished tiptoed back, but Erin was afraid to hold it too tightly. "Yes."

"Then come on," he said quietly. "I'll make us some."

Taking her robe from the hook on the back of the door, he held it, waited for her to leave the bed and slip her arms into it, then tied her sash.

Brimming with gratitude, she kissed his mouth. "I'll put on a pot of decaf."

"Do you have instant cocoa?"

"Cocoa? Yes, Christie likes it."

"Then let's have that instead. It's a cocoa kind of night."

She wasn't sure what made it a cocoa kind of night, and he didn't offer an explanation. But when he took her hand in his and led her to the kitchen, she knew she didn't need one.

The eggs were good—though she noticed him wince when she put ketchup on hers—and the cocoa was sweet on her tongue. But not as sweet as Mac's kisses after he accidentally knocked over the ketchup bottle and decided they should play spin the bottle for "favors." They laughed and teased like randy teenagers in a parked car...until the kisses and requests became more intimate and electric, and it got hard to breathe.

"I'd better get back to Amos's," Mac groaned hoarsely, skimming her body through her open robe and burying his face in her hair. "It's nearly midnight. If he wakes up, he'll wonder where I am."

"Or he'll know," Erin put in, tipping her head to give his slowly marauding mouth access to the throbbing pulse at her throat.

"'Night," he whispered. He nuzzled her collarbone, nuzzled her breasts before coming back to her lips.

"You taste like chocolate," she whispered moments later as they kissed and stroked their way into his room again.

Mac nudged the door shut with his bare foot, and they fell to the bed. His voice was low and trembling. "You taste like six weeks in heaven."

It was nearly impossible for Erin to temper her joy or the radiant smile she wore to Amos's the next morning, though she knew she had to try. The raw, whisker-burned spot on her chin—coupled with the happy glow she'd seen in the mirror when she awoke—was tantamount to putting an ad in the paper saying that Erin Fallon had been thoroughly, gloriously bedded the night before. So for privacy's sake, she did temper that smile, but inside there was a party going on.

He thought she tasted like six weeks in heaven.

"Good morning," she called, shepherding Christie inside and letting the back screen door shut behind her. Mac was just hanging up the phone in the kitchen, dressed for work in faded jeans and a black cotton shirt with the long sleeves rolled back. He looked sexy and dangerous, and her nerve endings curled as she recalled every heated touch, every murmur, every second of being held in his arms. "Hungry?" she teased in an undertone, expecting him to answer in kind.

When he didn't return her smile or tease back, she blamed it on Amos coming in from the living room. "Not particularly," Mac said. He motioned to the coffeepot. "I started the decaf. It's just about done."

His remote look and tone stopped her for a moment, then she told herself again that he was just being discreet, and was doing it badly. She smiled again. "Thanks. I'll pour you a cup when it's ready."

"Don't bother. I'll get it myself."

He'd get it himself? Erin stared at him in confusion and her pulse raced anxiously. What was going on? Why was he suddenly so distant? What had happened in the seven hours since he'd left her bed to make him act this way? Then half-a-dozen possibilities coalesced into one unshakable realization, and her heart shattered.

He'd finally gotten what he wanted. Now that the chase was over, she no longer interested him.

"Great," she said, fighting tears. "You do that." Then she turned away from him, started Amos's breakfast, and in time, worked up enough anger to burn away her misery.

For the next ten minutes Mac watched her set the table, pour coffee, stir oatmeal and chat with Amos and Christie as though nothing important had happened. If Amos had picked up on the tension between them, or noticed the whisker burn on Terri's cheek and chin, the old man kept it to himself. Mac was relieved. He wouldn't tell Amos the truth, and he didn't feel like making up a story.

Last night he'd let sex get in the way of getting the

answers he wanted. But he'd wanted more of her, and she'd wanted a moratorium on questions, and they'd both come away satisfied—then. Now he was furious at himself for deciding to accept her, secrets and all. Not that his resolve had lasted long. By the time he'd crashed in his old double bed upstairs, he'd known he couldn't live that way. Not after being married to the freaking Queen of Deception.

Walking to the sink, Mac drained his coffee cup, rinsed it, then returned to the table where Terri was wiping Christie's hands and face with a washcloth. "What's on the agenda today?" he asked as Amos carried his decaf into the living room.

The chill in her eyes could've stopped a bird in flight. "PT at one o'clock, then back here. Why?" she asked pointedly. "Do you *need* something from me?"

Holding back a curse, Mac listened for the clunk of Amos's recliner tipping back, then stepped closer to explain his mood. She'd shared nothing but her body with him last night, but being a hell of a nice guy, he would give her an explanation. Then Amos's recliner thumped down again, telling him his granddad was on the move once more, and he did swear—beneath his breath.

"No, I just wanted to remind you that I'll be meeting Shane tonight, so I won't be home for dinner."

"Fine," she answered, lifting Christie down from her booster chair.

"So glad you approve." Looking at her made him want her all over again, and that only increased his aggravation. "I'll be home to shower and change, but I'll be taking off right after that. Sophie's coming by around six, so you won't have to stay late."

She sent him another "Fine," and carried Christie's dishes to the sink.

Amos shuffled into the kitchen, his cane nowhere in evidence. "You boys stay away from them girlie clubs tonight."

"It's a business meeting, Granddad."

"It's monkey business if Shane's goin'," Amos returned. "He's a good egg, but that boy loves the women. Got himself in a pickle before, didn't he? Ended up needin' some penicillin."

Mac snatched his hat from the peg near the kitchen door. If he didn't get out of here soon, he'd have all the enamel ground off his back teeth. "He was nineteen and stupid, Granddad. Hopefully, he's a little brighter now. Have a good PT session." He hesitated on his way down the back porch steps and met Amos's gaze through the screen door. "Don't forget to ask Vicki about your working a few hours a week."

Amos lit up like a Roman candle. "First thing we'll be talkin' about. Have a good day."

"You, too." Tugging his Stetson low, Mac stalked to the store's old Chevy truck thinking sarcastically that it would be an absolutely *stellar* day. He still had no idea what he was going to say to Millie Kraft when he got her on the line, but by God, he *would* be talking to her today.

Erin rushed to the pantry and tried to pull herself together, but hot tears splashed over her lower lashes, and the racking sobs came. What had happened? Everything was fine when he left her last night! Why was he being so cold?

She sank back against one of the painted white posts that supported the shelves.

When would she ever learn that she was the world's worst judge of men? Hadn't her past relationships taught her *anything?* Grabbing a bunch of paper napkins from the bag on the shelf, she wiped her eyes and blew her nose. When it came right down to it, *were* all men alike?

She'd thought Mac was different. She'd trusted him, deluded herself into believing that there was something special between the two of them. Now she felt fragile and betrayed, and her lungs wouldn't work without pain.

Christie ran into the pantry, her eyes bright. "Bahney is on!" But a second later her tiny brows dipped uncertainly.

"I'm okay, sweetheart," Erin said, sniffing and shoving the napkins in the pocket of her jeans. She crouched for a hug. "I'm just getting the sniffles. Remember when you had them?"

Christie nodded vigorously. "Want to watch Bahney wif me and Papa Amos?"

"In a little while, honey. Mommy needs to finish the dishes."

"I will help!"

Erin's heart clenched as Christie ran into the kitchen, then scraped and dragged a chair noisily over the linoleum toward the sink. *Christie* was her future. She had to remember that. Mark had been a cheat, Charles had been a monster, and Mac...Mac was worse. Because of him, for a few hours, she'd let herself hope.

Millie Kraft's tone was cool and tentative. "I'm afraid I didn't get your name when you introduced yourself. Could you repeat it for me, please?"

"It's Corbett. Mackenzie Corbett."

"Thank you, Mr. Corbett. Now…why are you interested in obtaining a reference at this time if Terri's been working for you and your grandfather for a month?"

Mac withheld an irritated sigh. *He* was supposed to be asking the questions. "Because my grandfather apparently didn't make this call, and I need to know that the woman who's taking care of him is reliable and trustworthy."

"I see. Well, if you don't know the answer to that by now, then I can see why you thought this call was necessary. You're obviously not a very good judge of character."

Mac rubbed the headache brewing over his eyes. "Look—never mind about the reliable and trustworthy stuff. I guess I do know that about her. I just—I just need to know a few things. She says she's lived a lot of different places, and that makes me uneasy."

"It shouldn't. Not if you know she's trustworthy, and if her job is as temporary as you've said."

This was getting him nowhere. Better add some honesty. And in the blink of an eye, finally having to come up with an excuse for his questions told him why the answers were so damned important to him.

"Mrs. Kraft, I…I'm beginning to care about her, and for reasons I won't get into, I *can't* care about her before I know more about her past. I ask questions, and she either hedges or changes the subject."

The quiet reply on the other end of the line was a long time coming. "So you want me to tell you things that she won't?"

"Yes."

"I'm sorry. Friendships don't work that way. I will

tell you that she's a good girl. If you do care about her, give her some space. It took her nearly five months and a lot of coffee to open up to me.''

Mac waited, but Millie Kraft had finished speaking. ''That's it? That's all you can tell me?''

''That's it. Well, maybe one more thing. Her life hasn't been easy. So if she does let you in...you be good to her.''

Wonderful. He was nowhere closer to knowing her than he was before. ''Are you going to tell her I called?''

''No, she calls me. I don't know where she is, and I don't want you to tell me. But I think *you* should let her know that we've spoken.''

She didn't know where Terri was, and she didn't want him to tell her? What the hell...?

''Now if you'll excuse me, Mr. Corbett, I have customers.''

Mac sank back in his chair in the feed shed's small office, his mind shooting off in all directions. ''I'm sorry to keep you,'' he muttered. ''Thank you for your time.''

''You're welcome. Goodbye.''

Mac replaced the receiver. After a minute's thought, he glanced at his watch, mentally calculating the time between the next shipment, the start of Denny McCallin's one-o'clock shift, and Terri and Amos's departure for PT. His pulse picked up speed. He could easily get away from the store around noon if he had coverage and he was back in an hour.

He picked up the phone again. ''Denny, it's Mac,'' he said when Jeff Delaney's carrot-topped, teenage replacement answered the phone. ''Any chance you could come in an hour earlier today? I have a few errands to do, and I need someone down here at the Feed & Seed shed.''

''Sure!'' he said, obviously thrilled.

''Great. I'll see you at noon, then.''

''Yeah! See you at noon!''

Mac hung up, only slightly unsettled by what he was about to do. Despite Millie's advice to give Terri some space, he was through sitting on his hands. He'd given her ample time to ''let him in'' last night after they'd made love the second time, and she hadn't shared a damn thing. Not the reason for her ''sudden chill,'' not the slimmest scrap of information. Now he'd find those answers himself.

By 12:40 when he uncovered $13,000 in cash under the paper liner in Christie's pajama drawer, Mac's heart was pounding.

What in hell was she *into?*

Swearing again, he straightened the stack of pajamas and closed the drawer, then went to the kitchen, checked a number in the phone book and dialed. He hung up before it rang at the police station.

He couldn't ask Dave Kendall to check her out; what if she'd stolen the money and was running from the cops? Instantly he shook that thought from his head. Terri and handcuffs didn't even remotely go together. But if there was something in her past that she was running from, and the authorities were looking for her, Dave would be obligated to pick her up.

After another moment of indecision, he dialed Shane's sister Sally's number from memory. When Shane answered, he got right to the point. ''I need a favor. How good are your sister's computer skills, really?''

Shane laughed. ''So good we don't want the Feds to know about her. Why?''

''Can she…'' Mac hesitated, knowing he was asking a lot. ''Can she access certain databases?''

Shane didn't speak for a moment, then said cautiously, ''I suspect that depends on what kind of information you need and what you plan to do with it. What's going on?''

''Not on the phone. I'll tell you when I pick you up at six.''

Chapter 13

Sally Garrett rolled her chair back from her computer and shrugged. "Sorry. I tried several different spellings for Terri and for Teresa, but there's no woman by that name and approximate age in any of the databases I accessed." She turned to glance wryly at Mac, her chin-length brown hair swinging. "Found a guy named Terry in his early thirties, but I guess that won't help you much."

"Guess not," he replied. Maybe Terri was supposed to remain an enigma. Maybe fate or karma or whatever forces ruled the planets had decided he wasn't supposed to know anything about her.

"That doesn't mean she doesn't exist," Sally went on. "It only means that I can't find her—yet. Are you sure Teresa's her first name? I have a friend named Linda, but most people know her by her middle name—Susan."

"I don't know. Hell, the list of what I *do* know about her is damn short."

Sally's gray eyes softened. "Look, if you want, you can call me later with her license plate number. You could also check her owner's card and insurance information for her full name. Most people keep them in their vehicles in case they're stopped for a traffic violation. We'll see if any red flags pop up." She chewed her lower lip as she came to her feet. "But Mac—"

"Don't worry. I won't say anything to anyone. Believe me, this isn't something I'm proud of." The truth was, he was less proud of himself with each passing moment. Going through her things, digging into her friendship with Millie Kraft, asking Sally to access police files… He didn't get off on invading people's privacy, but dammit, he wasn't just ticked off at her. After finding that wad of cash, he was worried.

"You know," Sally reminded him, "if she moves around a lot that money's probably all she has. Why put it in a bank, if you plan to take it out again within a few weeks or months? Especially since some banks charge a penalty for early withdrawal. Cash is just easier."

"I know," he muttered. "I thought of that, too."

Shane came into the computer room, looping a tie around the raised collar of his white shirt. "Any luck?"

Mac shook his head. "You about ready to go?"

"Soon as I grab my jacket." Shane looked him over. "Sure you're still up for this?"

No, he wasn't, but Shane liked to eat well and they didn't get together that often. "Sure. Flagstaff's not that far. The Cottage Place okay?"

"Absolutely."

"Good." He glanced at Sally again. "Hey…thanks for your help, but I won't be calling you with her plate number or anything else. I'll get what I need from her."

"Good. That's the best way."

"I don't know if it's best, but it's more honest than what I've been doing. I'd appreciate it if you'd keep the things I've told you under wraps, too."

"Goes without saying," she replied, walking him and her brother to the door. "You like her, huh?"

"Maybe."

"Does she feel the same?"

Mac expelled a dry laugh as he and Shane descended the adobe bungalow's concrete steps to the walk. "Probably not if she's getting ready to leave."

Sally shrugged. "Well. Enjoy your dinner."

Mac called back his thanks, but dinner—even at The Cottage Place—wasn't appealing. Shane guessed as much as they pulled out of the driveway.

"Want to go someplace local and get drunk instead of driving to Flagstaff?"

"Sure, then I could really feel like garbage."

"Seriously. Let's skip dinner, lose the ties and jackets and go to Buster's. We can talk just as easily about the project there."

"You're not going to get charbroiled tiger shrimp at Buster's."

"No, but they've got pizza and beer, and that's good enough for me."

Mac looked askance at him. "Yeah?"

"Yeah."

The next morning, Mac decided that going to Buster's hadn't been one of his best ideas. His head pounded, his mouth felt like the bottom of a birdcage, and the impressive consumption record he'd racked up in college seemed to have dropped to four beers.

Amos didn't say a word when he walked, bleary-eyed into the kitchen, but he did stare in amusement as Mac went to the sink and knocked back some aspirin with water. Mac glanced Amos's way and scowled.

"I'm heading into the store early today," he grumbled, grabbing his Stetson. "Terri should be here in a few minutes."

"Lookin' forward to it. I need t'work on her some more."

Mac turned sharply and was instantly sorry as a wave of nausea hit him. He swallowed the sting of last night's pizza. "What are you talking about?"

"Sophie and me are headin' into town tonight to celebrate, and we want her and Christie to go along. You, too. Asked her last night, but she said that kinda thing was for family."

He took an orange from the fruit bowl on the table, then crossed to the wastebasket near the kitchen door to peel it. "'Course, we told her she and her little one *were* family." He glanced up. "So? You comin' over to the diner after you close up shop?"

"Sure. I'll see you around five-fifteen. What are we celebrating?"

"Me…graduatin' from PT."

Mac stifled a groan. He'd been so preoccupied with thoughts of Terri, he'd forgotten to ask Amos how things had gone. "Then you're finished?"

"Yup. They sprung me yesterday, so you might as well figure me into the schedule at the store. Vicki said it'll do me good t'get back in the saddle a couple hours a day.''

Mac spoke quietly. ''That's great, Granddad. But why don't you wait until tomorrow to come back? We can drive in together, and I'll take you home around noon. That way you can ease into things gradually.''

''I got no problem with that.''

The front screen door swung on its hinges, then shut noisily as Terri and Christie entered from the porch, Christie all smiles and running ahead, as usual.

Ruffling the toddler's hair as she ran past him, Mac watched Terri come through the hall to the kitchen. Even wearing a cool expression, she looked pretty in formfitting jeans and a light-blue knit top that clung to her curves. His interest increased when he noticed her hair.

She'd cut those grown-out bangs. Now her hair fell soft and black and feathery to her brows, framing the wide, intelligent blue eyes that continued to haunt his dreams. The remainder of her hair curved loosely around her shoulders. Very feminine, he thought. And as his libido caught up with his thoughts, it added, *very sexy*. If her gaze was a little less cold, he'd think the new hairstyle was due to his remarks at the canyon.

''Hi,'' he said. He'd never had a chance to explain his rotten mood yesterday, and he regretted that. But she'd owed him an explanation, too, so his regrets were minimal.

''Hi,'' she repeated flatly. She turned a smile on Amos. ''You look chipper today. Getting sprung seems to agree with you. What would you like for breakfast? Besides the fruit?''

With a wry twist of his mouth, Amos grabbed a napkin and his orange and limped into the living room.

"Since we both know I ain't gettin' sausages, whatever you fix'll be fine. Holler when it's ready. I'll be watchin' the news."

Mac met Terri's eyes when Amos was gone. None of the chill had left them. Turning away, she strode into the long, narrow pantry to drag out breakfast fixings. Mac followed and spoke in an undertone. "I had no right to treat you the way I did yesterday without letting you know why."

She snatched the oatmeal, napkins and syrup from a shelf. "Really?"

"Yes, really. When I got back here that night, things started eating at me." He glanced into the still-empty kitchen to make sure Amos was keeping his distance, then continued. "I thought we were going to talk after we made love the second time—but you still held back. Dammit, Terri, you have to be more open with me if this thing between us has a snowball's chance of going anywhere. That is, if you want it to go anywhere. I don't know if you do. Hell, I don't know if you're staying or going, or why you guard your privacy like Fort Knox. I don't know why you think you have to keep moving. I don't know who you are or what you're all about."

Her gaze fell. When it returned to him, her eyes were wary, and her voice trembled a little. "That's why you were so cold yesterday?"

"You thought I'd backed off because I'd finally gotten you into bed."

Her voice hardened again. "It crossed my mind."

"Terri, I don't make a habit of taking strangers to bed, and basically, after an entire month, that's what we are. Come to supper at the diner tonight. It would mean a lot to Amos. But afterward…we either talk or we end whatever's going on between us.''

The trapped look in her eyes when she finally nodded made him think of a condemned prisoner on her way to an execution. But he was through stumbling blindly through this relationship. He cared about her—too much, maybe—but there was no way to build on what they had without complete honesty.

Erin's stomach was queasy that evening as she and Christie sat with Sophie and Amos, scanning the diner's kids' menu. The restaurant was crowded, probably due to the banners in the windows and the daily-special flyers on the tables announcing that it was Tex-Mex night. Any other time, the spicy aromas of fried beef and chicken, tamales and hot peppers would've been welcome. Tonight, thinking about Mac's ultimatum, they made her nauseous.

Erin's nerves jolted as he walked inside looking rawly masculine in his black Stetson, black shirt and faded jeans. He waved and called to friends as he made his way back to their table. Mac took off his hat and set it on the chair beside him, then took a seat across from her and Christie.

''Hi, Unco Mac!''

''Hi, sweetheart.'' It was easy to see from the affection in his dark eyes how much Christie had come to mean to him.

But his look sobered when he met Erin's gaze. Still, there was intimacy there, too…and the banked needs of a lover remembering mind-bending kisses and heated touches. Erin couldn't help wondering if that look would disappear when she told him about her past.

Mac shifted a small plastic sombrero-and-cactus centerpiece aside and smiled at Amos and Sophie. "Did I see the two of you toasting when I came in?"

Amos chuckled. "We been doin' that since yesterday. You have a lot of catchin' up t'do, boy."

"Okay, then here's mine." He raised his water glass. "To my granddad, the most patient man in the county, who went through it all with a smile on his face and a good word for everyone."

Sophie expelled a hoot to the contrary, and Mac ended on a slightly more serious note. "Here's to seventy-three more years—of good health."

"Hear, hear," Erin said warmly, and they clinked glasses all around.

"So what's everyone having?" Mac asked, scanning the Tex-Mex flyer. "The carnitas and quesadillas are—"

"You gonna be able t'eat that spicy stuff after yer own celebration last night?" Amos chided through a chuckle.

A solid male voice behind him answered before Mac could. "Sure he will, Mr. Perkins. This guy's got a cast-iron stomach." The man's gaze shifted to Sophie. "How's it going, Mrs. Cassleback?"

A frisson of panic shot through Erin as Sophie answered that she was well—and Erin recognized the patrolman who'd stopped her for that bad brake light.

With an easy smile, Mac stood to shake hands. "You're way behind the times, buddy. My cast-iron stomach days are over." He nodded at Erin and Christie. "Dave, this is Terri Fletcher, granddad's housekeeper, and her daughter Christie. Terri—Officer Dave Kendall. We went to high school together."

Erin extended her hand to shake his and mumble,

"Nice to meet you," but her stomach was a jumble of butterflies. The condition got worse when recognition flickered vaguely in Kendall's eyes.

"Nice to meet you, too." He paused. "Terri, is it?"

Erin nodded and kept smiling, refusing to swallow the knot in her throat for fear of looking guilty. *Please, God, don't let him tell Mac about me. I need to do this myself or he'll never believe another word I say.*

"Terri's been with us more than a month now," Mac went on, then took his hat from the chair to his left. "Can you join us?"

Say no, Erin prayed.

"Thanks, but I'm with friends—cops' night out. I just stopped to say hello, and ask if you'd given any thought to that charity softball game I e-mailed you about a couple of weeks ago. Or didn't you get the message?"

Mac winced. "Yeah, I did. I just forgot about it. Sure, I'll play."

"Great. We can use your glove." He glanced across the room where two tables had been pushed together and a half-dozen men were laughing and talking with their waitress. "Well—looks like my food's arrived, so I'd better get back. But stop at my table on your way out so we can discuss the particulars. I'll be here for a while," he added wryly. "Those guys can eat."

When Kendall had said his goodbyes to Amos and Sophie, and his gaze met hers again, Erin felt a modicum of relief. If he thought she was familiar at first, he seemed to have changed his mind. "Nice meeting you, Ms. Fletcher."

"You too, Officer."

Her fajitas were probably good, but the butterflies never left Erin's stomach so she barely touched them.

She kept remembering with hope—and trepidation—Mac's words to her in the pantry this morning.

You have to be more open with me if this thing between us has a snowball's chance of going anywhere.

Did that mean he *wanted* it to go somewhere? Because that's what she wanted. Day by day she loved him more. But could she let their relationship grow, knowing that she could be putting him in danger? Charles would not be stopped. He had too much money and too much hate in him to imagine that he'd simply lose interest in taking Christie from her. And anyone who got in his way would pay a price.

Mac's voice rose as he stood and snatched the check the waitress had left. "I said I'm taking care of it, Granddad, so why don't you and Sophie just run along? I'll drive Terri and Christie home." Mac turned to her. "I do have to see Dave for a minute, though, so I'll meet you outside. There's a small playground out back. Christie might enjoy swinging for a few minutes."

Uneasy, but trying to reassure herself that Dave Kendall hadn't remembered her, Erin forced a smile. "Swinging might not be advisable after everything she ate, but yes, we'll wait for you there."

When Sophie and Amos had driven off in her big, flashy Edsel, Erin walked Christie across the parking lot to the playground, which was actually to the left and rear of the diner. A few other children and their parents had commandeered the swings and were happily calling to each other. But Christie was more interested in the sandbox near one of the three redwood picnic tables. Erin took a seat on the bench and watched her play.

They weren't there long when a dark-green van

pulled into the lot, and a man wearing jeans and a red-and-black-striped rugby shirt got out. He looked around, settled his sunglasses atop his blond surfer hair, then grabbed a map from his vehicle and walked toward her.

Erin's fears clicked in, and she moved from the table to sit in the grass near the sandbox. She shook off her suspicions a moment later when the man bypassed her and continued some distance away to speak to a father pushing his little boy on a swing.

She shook her head. Once again, she was being an alarmist; he was just a lost traveler. Would she never be able to look at a man in sunglasses again without getting anxious?

She turned her attention back to Christie, dug her hands into the sand and heaped more of it on the ''castle'' her daughter was building. But like the opportunities for happiness in her life, the sand kept sliding away, forcing her to work harder to make it stay.

''Uh—excuse me?'' a hesitant male voice said behind her.

Erin jerked around to see the young man with the map standing over her, and all of her senses went on full alert again. Although, with his easy smile and gentle manner, he didn't look like a threat.

''Yes?'' she replied, pushing to her feet.

His smile turned sheepish. ''I wonder if you could help me get back on Interstate 40. I'm on my way to California to meet my wife and daughters, and if I don't get straightened out soon, they'll be watching the Fourth of July fireworks without me.'' He nodded toward the dusky skinned man at the swings. ''I asked that guy over there, but I'm afraid my Spanish is worse than his English.''

When Erin didn't reply immediately, he sighed and grinned. "Actually...I don't even know what town I'm in."

Cautiously Erin took the map from his hand, then indicated a tiny dot on it. "You're here—in High Hawk. And the interstate isn't hard to find." She returned his map and nodded toward the road. "Take the first left after you leave the parking lot—you can see it from here—then make a quick right. That'll take you toward Flagstaff. You'll be able to pick up I-40 there."

His grateful smile pushed dimples into his cheeks. "Thanks. Hopefully I'll be better at this in my next life. Carole's usually the navigator, but her company transferred her to Barstow last month."

"You didn't go with them?"

He shrugged haplessly. "Nope. Somebody had to stay behind and sell the house." With a casual wave he backed away. "Thanks again—from all of us. I know macho guys don't say things like this, but it'll be good to see them again. E-mails and phone calls are nice, but hugs are better."

Erin couldn't disagree. "Travel safely."

"I'll sure try."

But as the man walked off, he stopped suddenly and slowly reversed his steps. "Hey—your little girl's about the same size as my Emily. Would you mind walking to my van with me for a second so I can hold the outfit I bought for her up against your daughter? Emmy'll be disappointed if it doesn't fit." He grinned again. "If you think I'm bad with directions, you should see me shop."

Alarms clanged in Erin's head, and she lifted Christie into her arms. "I'm sorry, I really don't have time.

We—we're waiting for my husband to come out of the diner."

The man stared back blankly for a second, then winced and lightly smacked himself in the forehead with his map. "I'm sorry. I scared you. That was a dumb thing for a stranger to suggest—especially someone with kids of his own. You and your family have a good day."

"You, too," Erin replied. But she still watched tensely until the van drove off before she took Christie's hand and walked her toward the diner.

Mac was just exiting when she and Christie arrived at the front door. Suddenly, just looking at him made her feel safe and secure.

It bothered her that he was unusually quiet on the ride home, and Erin found herself wondering if he was simply anticipating their discussion, or if he and Dave Kendall had talked about more than softball. But he didn't appear to be angry about anything, just... thoughtful.

Sophie and Amos were in the living room when they filed inside, talking over each other as they answered questions blaring from a game show on TV.

Amos called to them when they reached the kitchen. "You two oughtta sit down and watch this."

"I'd really like to," Erin replied, "but I have a thousand things to do. I just stopped in to congratulate you and thank you again for inviting me to your dinner party. It was fun."

"It *was* fun, wasn't it?" Sophie declared as the boxy-grinned game-show host called out another query.

"All right, panelists," he began, "here's your next

question. What did 100 people say that Americans value most in their lives?''

''Safety and freedom,'' Erin answered as she turned to leave. She caught Mac's gaze. His probing look after their quiet ride back home made her wonder again what he and Dave Kendall had talked about.

Tearing her gaze away, she gave Christie permission to stay with Papa Amos and Aunt ''Soapie'' for a while longer, then said her goodbyes.

Mac followed her out, his voice cool. ''Your answer surprised me.''

''Answer?''

''To that quiz-show question.''

''Oh?'' she returned, nervous now and feeling the tension between them growing. ''Why?''

''I'm not sure. You came up with 'safety and freedom' pretty fast. Don't you think stability is just as valuable? Particularly with a small child?''

He was angry now, and Erin increased her strides over the grass to the dirt lane, realizing that she'd had good reason to dread this talk of theirs.

''So tell me. Do you plan to keep dragging Christie from state to state for the rest of her life?''

Erin kept walking. ''Why are you getting into this again?''

''I know you love your gypsy lifestyle, but it's a bit immature, isn't it? Grown people make sacrifices for their children.''

Erin whirled on him, suddenly furious that he'd think for a moment that Christie wasn't her number-one priority. ''You have no idea what kind of sacrifices I've made for her!'' she shouted and continued walking.

"Then tell me!" he shouted back. His hand shot out to clamp her upper arm and spin her around.

Instinctively Erin dipped at the knees and raised her free hand to protect her face.

The look on his face was dumbfounded shock, and she straightened immediately.

Mac released her. "I wasn't going to hurt you. I would *never* hurt you." He scanned her face, and sick at heart, Erin looked away. "Has someone hurt you before? Your husband?"

Erin parted her lips to answer, but suddenly she was too humiliated to admit to the man she loved that she—an educated woman—had allowed herself to be manipulated into a relationship of fear. She was even more ashamed to admit that she hadn't been able to protect Christie from Charles's rage. She quickened her steps toward Mac's log home.

Swearing beneath his breath, Mac strode after her, his displeasure building again as Dave Kendall's words banged around in his mind. "All I know is, her name's not Terri Fletcher. It's Erin Fallon."

"You're positive?" Mac had said.

"Absolutely. I did a routine check when I picked her up on a brake-light violation. I always remember the pretty women I stop."

Gravel crunched beneath his boots as he swiftly came abreast of her again. "I can't take much more of this," he muttered. "We've made love. Twice. We've been as close as any two people can be. Haven't I earned your trust by now? You're the most secretive woman I've ever known—and after Audra, that's saying something. Why won't you tell me what's going on?"

"Mac, please, this isn't any of your business."

"I'm *making* it my business. Know what I've been doing the last few days? Checking you out. I know about the money in Christie's drawer. Is it stolen? Is someone after you?"

Erin lashed out, tears stinging her eyes. "You know about the money? You have the colossal gall to rain all over me about 'secrets' when you've searched through my things?"

"It was necessary."

"It was *not* necessary. It was an invasion of my privacy—that same privacy you swore you'd never breach. And I didn't steal that money. It's mine. I earned every last penny of it!"

She stormed up the stairs to his home, then stopped abruptly at the door. Turning around, she swiped angrily at her tears, pulled herself together and stared politely at him as he stood at the base of the steps. "Is this still my home for the next few hours?"

Mac felt himself turn to stone. "The next few hours?"

"Yes. We'll be leaving in the morning. Amos doesn't need me anymore."

It took a moment for him to answer. Then he nodded gravely. "Yes, Erin. It's still your home."

Thoughts and emotions he couldn't keep up with shot wildly through her gaze with his use of her given name.

"You need to stay away from me," she blurted out, her voice trembling.

"Let me help you."

"No! I don't want your help!"

"Erin—"

"I mean it, Mac!" she shouted. "Just leave me alone!"

That did it. That was enough for him. "Fine. I *will* leave you alone." What an idiot he'd been to think there could be a future with her. "You're just like Audra, closed and deceptive. Well, no more. Have a good life, Terri—or Erin, or whoever the hell you are. I'm through trying to break down your walls. I just don't have the energy for it anymore."

Another shock hit Mac when he strode inside Amos's place and heard his granddad and Sophie speaking in low tones in the kitchen. Curious, proceeding slowly through the hall, he picked up their conversation.

"...so I hope Davey Kendall kept quiet about it."

"But you heard him call her by another name?"

"Fallon. She thought I was sleepin' when he stopped her fer that brake light, but I heard him."

"And that's why you paid her in cash," Sophie murmured.

From the doorway, Mac saw his grandfather nod. "I figured a check with the wrong name on it could git her in more trouble than she was already in."

"Do you know what kind of trouble?" Sophie asked in quiet concern.

"Nope, but it can't be anything easy."

Incensed that everyone seemed to know more about her than he did, Mac walked into the kitchen. "Well, thanks a hell of a lot for telling *me* about this."

Amos jerked in surprise, then his expression evened out. "Now don't get yer blood up," he warned, "and keep yer voice down. Christie's colorin' in the parlor."

For Christie's sake, he did lower his voice, but Mac's frustration didn't ebb. "You've known, all this time, and you never told me?"

"You didn't want her here," Amos retorted defensively. "You wanted Mildred Manning. If you'da known, you mighta run her off, and I liked her."

"All right, but dammit, Granddad, why didn't you say something when you saw the two of us getting closer? I had a right to know."

"Because by then it was up to her t' tell you," Amos stated righteously.

Mac spun on his heel.

"Where you goin', boy?" Amos trailed him to the door. "If you press her fer an explanation before she's ready t' give it, you'll lose her."

"I'm not going to her."

"Well, thank the Lord fer that—not the way yer actin' now, anyways. Whether you know it or not, you need that gal."

"Right," Mac muttered. "I need another Mata Hari in my life." Letting the screen door bang shut behind him, he charged down the steps and across the grass to where his Cherokee was parked.

Roaring off, he headed toward town to see Dave Kendall about a woman named Erin Fallon who might or might not have been from Chicago. A woman he'd wanted so badly that he'd kept making excuses for her secrecy and silences to justify spending time with her.

A woman he'd fallen in love with.

Chapter 14

Heart pounding, Erin shut down the computer and rushed back to Christie's room. Fresh tears sprang to her eyes. She'd already packed most of their belongings, but she'd stopped before tackling Christie's things when she remembered she had to let Lynn know they'd be moving on again.

She hadn't written a word.

Lynn's reply to her earlier e-mail was on the screen when she booted up the computer.

Snatching Christie's clothes from the chest of drawers Mac had supplied, Erin stuffed them haphazardly into a plastic bag. Lynn had written:

I don't know how or when it happened, because Jeremy and I just got back from spending a month with my parents in Oregon. But I'm sure someone's been in my apartment, and I think that person has been accessing my e-mail. I've in-

stalled a firewall that should keep him out, but
your note to me wasn't protected, so there's a
chance someone knows where you are. Even I
know your general location after reading about
the place you and your friend visited.

I've tried to imagine another reason someone
might want to read my correspondence, but I
can't—maybe because I keep remembering
Charles's rage after I testified against him at the
custody hearing. He came by again after you left
Maine—in a rage again, and determined to find
you. Please, be careful! I'm praying for the two
of you, and hoping this new man can make you
happy.

Love always, Lynn

Erin's heart continued to beat doubletime. E-mail.
The blond man at the diner had mentioned e-mail.
He'd also worn sunglasses.

*One out of every three people you see here wears
sunglasses,* a voice in her mind countered sensibly,
*and half the world has e-mail. Those things mean noth-
ing.*

Not in and of themselves, Erin agreed, unwilling to
dismiss the intuitive feeling gripping her. But when
added to the stranger's behavior…maybe.

Had the man been playing a role? *Had* he been trying to snatch Christie, then, when Erin balked, feigned
that sheepish apology? In addition to that, the more
she racked her mind, examining everything he'd said
and done, the more certain she was that the father
pushing his son on the swing *had* spoken English.
She'd only heard a few words as she sat at the picnic
table—distant chatter to a child. But why would a man

use English with his son if he was more comfortable with Spanish?

Suddenly she knew she couldn't wait until morning to leave.

A soft rap sounded at the door.

Wiping her eyes, Erin rushed to the side light to peer out, then unlocked the inside and outside doors. Her heart squeezed with love when Christie catapulted herself into her arms.

"I missed you, Mommy!"

"I missed you, too, sweetheart," she murmured, lifting her and hugging her close. Erin's watery gaze moved to Sophie, who stared back in surprise, then helpless sympathy. The older woman took in the suitcases and bags sitting on the floor near the door.

"You're leaving," Sophie said quietly.

Erin nodded. Now, more than ever, she had to distance herself from this family she'd come to love. If any of her assumptions were true, she and Christie were at risk, and by association, Mac and Amos were, too. Even if she was wrong about the man at the diner, Mac had washed his hands of her, and she couldn't stay any longer, seeing the disillusionment in his eyes.

"Amos will be fine," Erin said. "He has you and Mac, and more importantly, he has himself. He's come a long way in the past five weeks. He doesn't need me anymore."

"And Mac?" Sophie asked hesitantly. "What about him?"

Erin's throat constricted. "Mac will be fine, too."

"Honey, I know he's upset right now. But no matter what he says or how he acts, he cares—a lot more than he'll even admit to himself."

"Then that's all the more reason for me to leave. I can't give him what he needs."

Erin saw Christie's lower lip tremble, and she quickly reassured her. "Just more sniffles, honey," she said with a smile. "Mommy's fine." She met Sophie's eyes again, and reluctantly told another half lie. She needed to expedite their departure, but she couldn't leave without letting Amos know she would contact him. "I should finish packing if we're going to leave in the morning. Please tell Amos we'll say our good-byes tomorrow."

But they would do it by phone when they were on their way. She couldn't do it in person and let him try to dissuade her. That could be dangerous for all of them. Or not. Again she wondered if there would ever be a time when fear and uncertainty didn't rule her world.

Tears shone in Sophie's eyes now, too. "Then I'll say goodbye now since I'll be heading for home."

Sophie was leaving? "Then…Mac's back?" A tiny part of her clutched that news as if there were still a chance for them.

"Not yet. He phoned a while ago to say he'd be home soon, though. But Amos has already turned in, so I'm leaving." She forced a smile. "Tomorrow's a big day for him. He'll be a working man again, and he wants to be well rested."

Sophie opened her arms and hugged them both. "Goodbye, honey. I know we haven't known each other long, but I care about you. Godspeed."

"You too, Sophie."

Ten minutes later Erin had rocked Christie to sleep in her street clothes, settled her on the couch and was hurriedly finishing her packing. Mac's accusing tone echoed in her mind as she tucked their cash inside Christie's Barbie satchel. He'd thought she could be a thief—as well as a liar.

Again the thought of leaving him brought tears, but she blinked them back. She just hoped that someday he could forgive her for not being honest with him when she had the chance.

She'd left her van parked beside the house instead of pulling it up close to the porch steps, so Amos wouldn't see her packing it. Now, leaving the porch light out and depending on the rectangles of light from the windows to see, Erin carried their two suitcases into the darkness, the night air cool on her stinging eyes.

How many people knew about her by now? she wondered, opening the back of the van and shoving the suitcases inside. Dave Kendall without a doubt. Sophie and Amos, probably. And some of the officers at the restaurant if Kendall and Mac hadn't been discreet.

She hurried back to the house for their duffle bags, then retraced her steps quickly to the van.

If just one of those people told someone about her, the rumor mill would handle the rest. If Charles *had* sent someone to find them, they would be found soon.

Galvanizing herself, she returned to the house for Christie's toys, clothes and sleeping bag and stuffed them in among the suitcases and duffels. She just needed to grab Christie's portable bed rail and leave a note for Mac.

Tears welled again at the finality of what she was about to do. How could she leave him when she loved him so much it hurt to imagine a life without him?

The answer came quickly and gave her strength: because your daughter deserves to grow up happy and free.

Hurrying back inside, she checked to see that Christie was still asleep, then turned off the light in the great room and strode into Mac's office for pen and paper. She had no idea what she would say, other than to thank him for his generosity and his kindness. Telling him about Charles wouldn't accomplish a thing now.

The door creaked behind her just as she clicked on the small lamp over the desk. Terror splintered through her when Erin whirled around.

The blond man who stepped out from behind the door sent her a friendly smile as he pulled a garrote from his jacket pocket. "Hello again, Mrs. Fallon. Thanks for the directions this afternoon. But," he added with an amiable shrug, "I decided not to go to Barstow after all."

Mac sat in Amos's driveway in his idling Cherokee, watching the lamps go out in his great room. She was going to bed. He rubbed the tension over his eyes.

He wanted to talk to her, yet he was still emotionally shackled by what he'd learned tonight. Why couldn't she have trusted him enough to tell him about her past? Dammit, he would have understood. She'd made a mistake, but she'd rectified it.

From the information Kendall'd been able to gather, and the little Mille Kraft had reluctantly told him tonight, he'd pieced together a scenario that, by turns, made him sick and filled him with an overwhelming urge to pound Charles Fallon into the pavement.

Thank God Erin had drawn a sympathetic judge for the second custody hearing, and the creep had been denied any further contact with Christie.

What kind of man could slap his nineteen-month-old daughter—then knock her to the ground—for something as insignificant as spilling juice on his trousers? And amazingly, Fallon had had the ego to do it during a supervised visit in a park where others could see him!

Mac left his car and climbed the steps to Amos's place, glancing at his house again—a house that had become a home with Erin and Christie in it. The smells of good things baking, the warmth of scented candles, the sounds of loving conversations and high pitched giggles had all combined to make a rambling dwelling into a place he wanted to spend time.

He had to convince her not to leave tomorrow morning.

Sighing, Mac went inside, then reached down to pull off his boots.

He jerked upright again when the intercom crackled, and Erin's strident voice sliced through the air.

"—don't care what you do to me, but please don't let Charles have Christie. He's a monster! He'll hurt her! He'll destroy her spirit and turn her into a—"

"Sorry. Nothing personal, but moneybags wants you dead and his daughter back. And I want the rest of my fee."

Sheer terror razed Mac's nerve endings as he bolted from the house and down the porch steps, praying for her life—praying for all of their lives because he had none without her.

He ran through the darkness like a man possessed, his heart thundering in his chest, the moon shedding only a glimmer of light through the trees. Then he was up the steps, crossing the porch and throwing open the screen door—not giving a damn for the noise he made.

Mac burst into the computer room just as a blond man threw Erin to the floor and yanked a gun from his waistband.

This wasn't real! It was a scene from a movie!

Mac lunged for him in an all-out tackle, and they crashed into the storage boxes and fell to the floor, boxes toppling onto them. The intruder kicked and clawed at him, but Mac managed to stay on top. Then he angled a gun at Mac and fired twice!

Erin screamed as the shots went wild.

"Get Christie out of here!" Mac shouted, clamping the assassin's wrist, fighting for the gun, smashing it against the floor to dislodge it. The assassin's free fist found Mac's kidney at the same time he squeezed off another round.

Mac gritted his teeth, banged harder on the gun. It skittered between two cartons, but the intruder found new strength, throwing Mac off him and scrambling to his feet. He bolted into the foyer and out the door.

Mac sprang to his feet and through the door, lunged at the man again, knocking him down. They skidded across the porch, tumbled down the steps to the grass. Mac got to his feet first. The blonde kicked for his knee and missed. They were both on their feet now, exchanging blows and warding off punches. Then bellowing with the effort, Mac smashed his fist into the assassin's jaw.

The man crumpled like a stringless marionette.

For a long moment, Mac stood weaving over him, gasping and waiting to see if the man would move again. Praying he wouldn't. Then, still breathing hard, he slipped his belt from his belt loops and crouched to lash the man's hands behind his back.

He was just rising when Amos came toward him at

a hobbling run, brandishing a shotgun. "I heard it all!" he shouted, gasping for breath, his voice shaky. "Cops're on their way." In a moment he was beside Mac and staring down at the unconscious man. Amos pressed a hand to Mac's back. "You okay, boy?"

Mac squeezed his grandfather's shoulder. "Yeah, Granddad. I'm okay."

A car door slammed, and both men looked toward the sound. Erin was hurrying across the grass to them, carrying Christie.

"In fact," Mac said through a sigh, "I think we're all going to be okay now."

With his heart sagging in relief, he strode forward to meet them and wrap them in his arms.

Two patrol cars were there in minutes, sirens screaming. The team in the first one quickly took the intruder into custody, notified the ambulance en route that there'd been no injuries, then drove off with their prisoner. Dave Kendall and his partner stayed behind to take their statements.

Now, with a wave at Kendall's departing vehicle, Mac trudged up the steps to his home and went inside.

He smiled a little when he glanced through the hall to the kitchen and saw Amos making cocoa.

Cocoa. Fixer of all things gone wrong.

Erin was still on the sofa in the great room, and still holding Christie close, even though the little girl had fallen asleep. After hearing the story she'd told Kendall, Mac didn't blame her.

It still pricked a little that he'd had to hear about her life at the same time the police and Amos had.

Wandering into the room, he took a seat beside her on the sofa. She looked tired, drained...and still so incredibly beautiful that it staggered the mind.

He sat there for a while, not touching her, wanting to ask a hundred questions, yet knowing this wasn't the time. She needed to regroup. A few words slipped out, anyway. "I wish you'd told me. I might've been able to help."

Her eyes filled with regret. "That's exactly why I couldn't tell you. I would have been putting you and Amos at risk, too. As it happened, you were already on Charles's list."

Tears welled, but she managed to hold them back. "I'm so sorry, Mac. For lying to you, for…for not trusting you. For everything." Her voice caught. "You could've been killed tonight."

"But I wasn't."

"Only by the grace of God. That man would have come for you. He told me so. Charles wanted us both dead. I don't know how he found out about us, but he knew. And Christie… He would have delivered Christie to Charles, and her life would've been a nightmare."

Mac's anger surged as he recalled what Fallon had done to Christie, but he remained outwardly calm. "Again, that didn't happen."

The phone rang. Amos's gravelly "Hello" carried to them from the kitchen. A moment later he came into the room, carrying two cups of cocoa. "Phone fer you, Mac," he said, putting the mugs down on the coffee table. "Davey Kendall."

Mac glanced at the mugs. "Where's yours?"

Amos nodded toward the kitchen. "Out there."

"Then you take this one," he insisted, moving a cup to the end table beside his overstuffed brown recliner. "I'll grab the other one after I take Dave's call." He smiled when his grandfather plunked himself into the chair, touched again by the old man's love and his bravery in trying to come to their rescue tonight. "Thanks, Granddad."

"Fer what? It ain't hard t'make cocoa."

Mac gave his shoulder an affectionate squeeze before he left the room. "I'm not talking about the cocoa. I'm talking about the shotgun."

When Mac returned several minutes later, Erin was holding her mug in both hands, Christie was curled up, asleep, on the couch, and she and Amos were immersed in a low conversation. Mac lounged in the archway with his own cocoa to listen.

"After the people who saw Charles hit Christie testified at the hearing, the judge declared him unfit and awarded me full custody. Charles went crazy. I had a restraining order against him, but he shoved his way through the crowd in the hall and told me he would use whatever means he needed to get her back. He said she belonged to him, and there was nothing I or the courts could do about it. I knew he had enough money to make it happen. That's when my friend Lynn and I decided I had to disappear."

Mac gritted his teeth but kept silent.

"I knew Charles would have us followed. So I left my car in the long-term parking lot at the airport and went inside to buy two tickets to New Orleans. Then, when it was nearly time for our flight, Christie and I met Lynn and her two-year-old son in the ladies' room. When Lynn and Jeremy got on the plane, she was wearing my sunglasses, jacket and floppy hat, and her little boy was dressed in Christie's clothes. They flew to New Orleans in our place."

She stared into her cocoa for a moment. "I'd given her enough cash to book a return flight the next day in her own name. In the meantime, Christie and I took a cab to a bus depot. The rest reads like an atlas of small towns and cities from Iowa to Maine.''

Mac straightened in the doorway and walked to her. ''That's where the private investigator found you?''

She nodded. ''We'd stayed there too long—five months—a lot longer than we'd stayed anywhere before.'' She sent him a beaten look. ''But I was so tired of running, and I'd made friends again—*good* friends.''

''Like Trisha,'' Mac said, remembering the story she'd told Kendall.

She nodded sadly.

''And y' had to become somebody else,'' Amos put in.

Erin nodded again. ''Terri. My best friend from high school. She died after contracting meningitis when we were seniors.'' She sent Mac a look that asked his forgiveness. ''I felt terrible using her name. But I'd bought this book over the Internet, and—among other things—it said if someone really wanted to disappear, they'd need a social security number that wasn't being used anymore. I took Terri's.''

Amos scowled. ''Well, now that that blond yahoo's locked up, you can stop runnin'.''

But there was doubt in her eyes. ''Can we?''

Mac crouched beside her. ''Yes. You can. Apparently by the time Mr. Smith—probably not his real name—made it to the jail, he'd agreed to testify against your ex in return for a deal. They're working with the prosecutor's office on it right now. Dave says it shouldn't be long before the Chicago PD relieves Fallon of his Rolex and ushers him into his new eight-by-eight condo.''

"But how long can they keep him there?"

"I don't know," Mac replied honestly. "But Dave said the list of things they can charge him with are stacking up. Attempted murder, conspiracy, attempted kidnapping and reckless endangerment for starters. Erin, he'll be making license plates and turning big rocks into little rocks for a long, long time."

"And now," Mac added, "Granddad and I are going to take off and let you and Christie get some sleep."

Suddenly fear gripped her again. Moistening her lips, she said hesitantly, "Would you mind staying here tonight?" She glanced at Amos. "You, too. I...I know this is silly, but I could sleep in the twin bed with Christie, and—"

Mac didn't let her finish. "Sure. I'll crash on the couch. Granddad can have the bedroom."

Grunting to his feet, Amos declined. "Thanks, but I'm goin' up home. I sleep better in my own bed. Besides," he said with a faint smile, "I expect you two got some things to talk about."

"I'll walk you to the house," Mac said.

Erin crossed to Amos and wrapped her arms around him, kissed his cheek. She was touched when he returned her hug. "Thank you, Amos," she murmured. "For everything." Then, stepping back, she said to Mac, "Take my van. The keys are still in the ignition."

He nodded. "I'll see you in a few minutes." Then he bent and kissed her softly, breaking her heart all over again.

He didn't sleep on the couch.

They made love in his bed, and it was poignant and

sweet, tender and exciting, all at the same time. A wonderful celebration of life after nearly losing it. Erin gloried in each touch and caress, tucking them into a corner of her heart and committing them to memory because she knew it would never happen again.

They were lying in each other's arms in the near darkness, their bodies sated, their hands softly stroking, when Mac murmured, "Marry me."

Erin stilled, then reluctantly moved her fingers from his chest. "You don't mean that. It's just the night talking."

Mac stacked their pillows against the headboard, then gathered her in his arms again and lay back. He smoothed her hair from her cheek, then tipped her face up to him and kissed her. "No, it's not the night talking. I love you…and I think you love me."

Erin's heart swelled, but no matter how welcome his words were, they weren't enough. "I've had two disastrous relationships, Mac."

"Third time's the charm, right?" When she didn't reply, he went on. "What do you think will happen, Erin? Do you think I'll turn into a cheat like Mark or a megalomaniac like that freak in Chicago?"

"No!" She drew a breath and tempered her reply. "No. You could never be like him."

"Thank you. But if you know that, there has to be another reason you won't say yes. What is it?"

Moving out of his arms, she drew her legs to her chest, the sheet tenting over her knees. "How can you love and respect a woman who put her child at risk and allowed herself to be treated like—"

"Because that woman is you. And because you left the son of a bitch when you realized what you'd gotten yourself into."

''He hurt Christie.''

''During a supervised visit monitored by someone else. And that wasn't your fault or your friend Lynn's. Erin, put the blame where it belongs.''

''But I picked him.''

''No, you *left* him.''

Mac pulled her close again. He felt warm and solid, strong and safe. ''What else?'' he prompted.

She swallowed. ''I'm afraid that I've lied so much and so often that you'll never be able to trust me completely—not after two women you cared about lied to you. Mac, I couldn't handle seeing the doubt in your eyes if I stayed.''

''Erin—''

''Love and trust go hand in hand. Without trust, love can't last.'' She paused, drew a breath. ''You said I was like Audra.''

''Yes, I did. And at the time I meant it. But there are no more secrets between us now.'' He turned her face up to his again, and in the meager moonlight through the windows, she saw a flicker of uncertainty in his gaze. ''Are there?''

That tiny moment of doubt sealed her resolve and crushed any lingering hope that they had a future. ''No,'' she whispered. ''You know everything about me now.''

''Then say yes.''

She shook her head. ''You might not know it now, but there'll come a time when you'll have doubts. You'll wonder if what I tell you is the truth or just my version of it.''

''You're wrong.''

''I don't think so.''

"Then where does that leave us?" he asked, but there was a subtle difference in his tone.

Erin kissed him softly, then moved out of his arms to sit again. "Mac, my...my van's already packed... and my father has never met Christie. Heaven knows he was never a doting parent, but time changes people, and Christie deserves to know her grandfather. It could be a second chance for all of us. We're leaving for San Diego in the morning."

She heard the rustle of sheets behind her, felt the mattress dip as he sat up, too. The change in his voice became more pronounced. "So what was tonight?" he challenged.

"Tonight was a wonderful gift that I'll treasure forever. Can't you see that I'm doing this for you?"

Mac swung his legs over the edge of the bed and settled his feet on the floor. "I'm going back to Amos's. You were wrong before, Erin. You're not afraid to be alone. You want it that way."

"That's not true," she said in a rush. "No one wants to be alone. It just turns out that way sometimes."

He never said another word to her. He simply got out of bed, dressed and left.

The California sun was high in the sky three days later when Erin drove her van back to the white stucco motel's blacktopped parking lot. The palm trees waving along the street and the fragrant bougainvillea clustered near the glass-paned office made their accommodations look a lot more elegant than they were. Still, their second-level room was neat, clean and had served its purpose.

Slinging her leather bag over her shoulder, Erin got

out of the van, plucked Christie from her car seat and set her on her feet. Then, taking her hand, she slammed the van's side door and walked her toward the black metal steps leading to their room.

"Tired, sweetie?"

"No, I'n hungry."

Erin forced a smile, still feeling the sting of their disastrous visit. "We'll get a cookie and some juice when we get to our room. That should tide you over until dinnertime." There'd been nothing offered at her father's apartment.

John Michael O'Rourke was still the same indifferent man her mother had divorced. The same cavalier Irishman who'd left them to pursue his sun-and-surf dream. He'd had a woman at his cramped, stucco apartment eight streets from the beach, and she'd been tanned and blond and much closer to Erin's age than her father's. In the blink of an eye, he'd shuttled her and Christie outside to his cheap concrete balcony, then winked and admitted he didn't want Sherry to know he was a grandfather.

Christie said something she didn't hear, and Erin looked down at her daughter. "What, honey?"

"Unco Mac has ice cweam."

But Uncle Mac was hundreds of miles away. Erin held back a sigh. If there was a heavier heart in the nation, she didn't know who it belonged to. "Maybe we can find a nice ice cream shop around here." Then she lifted her gaze again…and her heart stopped beating.

A burgundy Cherokee with Arizona plates was pulled up to the office door. Erin felt a rush of adrenaline. It couldn't be.

But it was. She recognized his blue-plaid shirt as

Mac pushed through the glass door and strode out onto the walk, recognized his broad shoulders and the sure, confident way he carried himself.

She tried to calm her runaway pulse as he turned away from them and into the U-shaped motel complex. Then, suddenly, some sixth sense must have told him to turn around, and he did.

Their gazes locked.

Slowly he walked to her, his black Stetson shading his face, his long, denim-clad legs gradually eliminating the distance between them.

"Unco Mac!" Christie shrieked.

"Hi, shortcake," he said, grinning at her for a moment before his gaze sobered and rebounded to Erin.

"How did you find us?" she asked quietly.

"It wasn't easy," he replied in the same low tone. "I've been combing motels and hotels in San Diego since last night." He paused. "How did it go with your dad?"

Erin shrugged, knowing her hurt probably showed. "Not as well as I'd hoped. Pretty badly, actually."

Mac shook his head. "When are you going to stop running away and run to me? All your life you've been looking for a home, first with a father who didn't want you, then with an unfaithful fiancé, then with that freak in Chicago—who is now behind bars, I'm glad to say."

Mac reached for Christie and hoisted her onto one arm. He opened the other to Erin. "Don't you know where home is?" he asked quietly. "It's here. With me. You and Audra are worlds apart. She was deceptive because it was her nature. You did what you had to do to keep your daughter safe. Why do you think I can't understand and accept that?"

He opened his arms a little wider. "I love you and I trust you. Nothing will ever change that."

Erin rushed to him, casting all doubt aside, so grateful for second chances and so filled with joy the word paled compared to her feelings. "I love you, too," she whispered, hugging him fast. "Oh, Mac I *do* love you."

His kiss was swift and thorough, sweet enough to melt her heart, yet deep enough to chase any doubts from Erin's mind. She would love this man until the day she drew her last breath…and then she would love him a little longer.

Easing from the kiss, Mac smiled down at her. And Erin saw the same promise of forever in his eyes. Then he kissed Christie's nose, hugged his family close again and murmured, "Come on. Let's go home."

Epilogue

Blissfully contented with the day, but tingling with excitement for the night to come, Erin watched from the porch as her husband spoke through the open window of Shane's SUV and said a second goodbye to his new partner.

Voluminous white dining tents and netting still fluttered in the deepening dusk, with a profusion of tiny lights and ivy, pink roses and white organdy ringing the pond and festooning the lattice arbor where their ceremony had taken place. Even elderly Reverend Henderson had marveled that the woodland expanse between their home and Amos's looked like a fairy-tale setting.

Shane hit the key, and the SUV sprang to life, and Erin smiled in expectation…because Mac was slowly backing away, tall and lean and handsome in his black tuxedo, even though his tie had been gone and his collar open since their I do's.

Millie, who'd given her away, Lynn, her matron of honor, and cute little Jeremy, who'd been their ring bearer, had left shortly after their other guests. And minutes ago Christie had gone off in her flower-girl gown to spend the night with "Aunt Soapie" and Papa Amos, who would marry next weekend.

She remembered Amos's shiny eyes when Mac asked him to be his best man. "Not Shane?" he'd asked gruffly. "No," Mac had replied, smiling. "Shane's a good friend. But you're the best man I know."

"See you Monday," he called now as Shane drove off. Then, flashing her a smile, Mac said, "Don't move. I'll be right back," and loped off to unplug the twinkle lights.

They'd chosen to postpone their honeymoon trip until later with Mac's and Shane's business just getting started. Besides, after all their wanderings, Erin was more than content to stay home.

Home.

If anyone had told her in June that her life would take such an extraordinary turn by the middle of August, she wouldn't have believed it.

But now Charles was in a jail, and the man who'd called himself John Smith was in Maine, waiting to stand trial for Trisha's murder.

Mac came bounding up the steps to spin her around, her white gown billowing. His smile was broad and eager and his dark eyes were full of mischief. "You're wearing too many clothes."

"So are you," she laughed, then shrieked when he scooped her into his arms and lifted her in a rustle of organdy and silk. Erin wrapped her arms around his neck.

"Ready to start our life together, Mrs. Corbett?" he murmured, opening the door.

Erin's eyes stung with happy tears. "You bet, Mr. Corbett."

"Great," he said, grinning again. "Let's go make a baby brother for Christie."

Then, laughing and kissing, they crossed the threshold to their future.

* * * * *

Silhouette®

COMING NEXT MONTH

INTIMATE MOMENTS

#1273 DOWNRIGHT DANGEROUS—Beverly Barton
The Protectors
Cleaning up the seedy underbelly of Maysville turned out to be
a downright deadly proposition for Elsa Leone—that is, until
Dundee agent Rafe Delvin was hired to watch her back. As the
Dixie heat riled the town, Rafe found himself drawn to Elsa's
passionate nature—but would he be able to stop her attacker?

#1274 DANGEROUS GAMES—Marie Ferrarella
Cavanaugh Justice
Wealthy builder Cole Garrison knew his younger brother was the
victim of a police cover-up. And with time running out, Cole put
his trust in maverick detective Lorrayne Cavanaugh to solve the
mystery. But would the trail of secrets lead them to each other…
as well as the killer's identity?

#1275 CROSSFIRE—Jenna Mills
Bodyguard Hawk Monroe wanted to break Elizabeth Carrington's
cool society facade. She'd walked away from him before…but now
a threat to her life brought her back. Despite the danger lurking,
Hawk planned to use every *heated* moment to recapture the passion
they'd once shared.…

#1276 THE CRADLE WILL FALL—Maggie Price
Line of Duty
Sergeant Grace McCall still remembered the searing passion she'd
once shared with FBI agent Mark Santini, but his job had torn them
apart. Brought together again on an undercover assignment, the duo
had to pretend to be married to catch a killer preying on kids.
Would their make-believe partnership turn into a lifetime union…?

#1277 SWEET SUSPICION—Nina Bruhns
Federal witness Muse Summerville knew agent Remi Beaulieux
would keep her alive—and locked away in a bayou cottage
under his *protective custody,* and she found it impossible to resist
their mutual attraction. Yet, before long the duo had to face the New
Orleans crime boss threatening to tear them apart…forever.

#1278 UNDERCOVER VIRGIN—Becky Barker
Lone-wolf operative Kyle Tremont wasn't prepared to handle
the vixen he'd been asked to rescue. After her cover had been
compromised and she was forced on the run with Kyle, FBI
agent Rianna Sullivan thought she'd lost her chance to avenge
her family's murder. Would his love be enough to stop her vow
of revenge?

SIMCNM0104